AN HEIR
CLAIMED BY
CHRISTMAS

D1345082

AN HEIR
CLAIMED BY
CHRISTMAS

CLARE CONNELLY

MILLS & BOON

First published in Great Britain 2020
by Mills & Boon, an imprint of HarperCollins*Publishers*
1 London Bridge Street, London, SE1 9GF
www.harpercollins.co.uk

HarperCollins*Publishers*
1st Floor, Watermarque Building, Ringsend Road
Dublin 4, Ireland

Large Print edition 2021

© 2020 Clare Connelly

ISBN: 978-0-263-28844-5

MIX
Paper from
responsible sources
FSC **FSC™ C007454**

Printed and bound in Great Britain
by CPI Group (UK) Ltd, Croydon, CR0 4YY

For readers of romance and lovers of Christmas—some of my favourite people!

And for the real-life Dimitrios—thank you for inspiring the name of my hero.

PROLOGUE

'WHAT EXACTLY AM I looking at?' Dimitrios's scorn for journalists was evident in the tone of his voice. Always somewhat intimidating, he reserved a particularly gruff response for the man on the other end of the phone.

'My email?' The reporter's smugness was unbearable.

Its subject was: Call me to discuss.

The only text in the email read:

Article running in the weekend papers.

Attached was a photograph of a young boy.

It was a bizarre enough email to prompt Dimitrios's response. There was something in the child's face—his eyes—that was familiar to Dimitrios, and a spark of worry ignited.

His twin brother, Zach, was renowned for his startlingly brief affairs. Was it possible he had, somewhere over the years, fathered a child?

It was just the kind of scandal the papers would love, dragging their family name—and that of the media empire Zach and Dimitrios had worked their backsides off to protect since inheriting the multi-billion-dollar corporation from their father—through the mud.

'Is there another reason I would have called you?'

Ashton worked for a rival newspaper based out of Sydney. Dimitrios could have—and would have—pulled strings to have the story killed in his own papers but he knew nothing he said would deter Ashton.

'So? Do you have a quote?'

Dimitrios sighed. 'How can I? I have no idea what response your cryptic photograph is supposed to elicit from me. Recognition? Fear? Sorry to disappoint, but I feel neither.'

He would need to speak to his brother, find out if he knew anything about this. Surely Zach would have mentioned having had a child? Unless he didn't know? Although, wasn't it far more likely this journalist was grasping at straws?

'What about if I give you the name Annie Hargreaves?'

Dimitrios's whole body responded. Staring out

of the window of his top-level office at the morning sun that coated Singapore in a golden glow, past the iconic towers of Marina Bay Sands towards the strait, he felt as though a rock had been dropped on his gut.

'What did you say?'

The question was asked through bared teeth. He didn't need Ashton to repeat the question. Everything about Annabelle Damned Hargreaves was burned into his memory. Her body. Her kiss. Her innocence. The way she'd looked at him the night they'd made love, as though it had meant something important, something special. As though he could have given her anything— as though he were that kind of man! Instead of understanding what it actually had been—an outpouring of mutual grief after the death of his best friend, her brother.

He thought of the things he'd said to her after they'd slept together, after he'd taken her virginity. Words that even at the time had been calculatedly cutting. He'd followed the old adage of being cruel to be kind, understanding that she wanted more from him than he would ever be able to give. Knowing he needed to destroy any childish fantasies and hopes she might have had that he, Dimitrios Papandreo, could be the kind of man to give her some kind of mythical happily-ever-after. He'd never been that way inclined but, after Lewis's death, the reality of life's cruelty had been made abundantly clear to him.

None the less, having her name come out of nowhere sent a pulse of raw feeling through his body, scattering any ability to think rationally. Every one of his senses went on high alert in a response that was pure survival instinct.

'Miss Annie Hargreaves, twenty-five years old, of Bankstown, Sydney. Six-year-old boy. Single mother to a little boy named Max. Now do you care to comment?'

Dimitrios gripped the phone more tightly, his whole body coursing with a type of acid. His gut rolled, every muscle on his lean, athletic frame tensed as though he were preparing for a fist fight.

Six.

Max.

The facts exploded through him like sticks of dynamite.

He swore inwardly, standing abruptly and stalking towards the windows, bracing one arm against the glass, pressing his forehead to it, staring directly beneath him. The sense of vertigo only compounded the spinning feeling he was already combatting.

Lewis had died seven years earlier. The anniversary of his death had just passed—a day Dimitrios and Zach marked each year. The three of them had been inseparable, more than best friends. Lewis had been like a third brother. His death had destroyed Dimitrios and Zach. His loss had been shocking—how someone so healthy and strong could simply cease to exist, all of his life force and energy just…gone. Dimitrios had known pain in his life, but never that kind of grief, and it had torn him in two.

His eyes swept shut as he thought of Lewis's little sister.

Annabelle…

It wasn't possible.

'Rumour has it you two hooked up one night, about nine months before this little boy was born.'

Rumour? No. A source. There was no rumour about a child of his or he would have heard it much sooner. Somehow, this man had been given the information from someone who knew way too much.

Annabelle?

He rejected the idea immediately. If she'd wanted anyone to know, she would have come directly to him. Wouldn't she?

'Don't you get it, Annabelle? I was drunk. I came here because I was thinking about Lewis, and I was missing him, and I wanted to talk to someone who would understand. That—' he'd pointed to the bed '—was never meant to happen. I would never choose to go to bed with you. Surely you can see that?'

'So?' Ashton pushed. 'Any confirmation? Have you met your son, Dimitrios?'

His son. It was as if the dynamite kept sparking and exploding, reigniting and exploding all over again. His arm took most of his body weight. His symmetrical face looked as though it had been sculpted with a blade. Tension radiated from his pulse points.

'Look after her for me, Dim. Annie's going to be devastated. She won't cope with this. Please check in on her. Make sure she's okay.'

Guilt nauseated him, as always. The sense that he'd failed his friend, and broken the death-bed promise Lewis had extracted from him, all because grief had driven his body to seek consolation in the one way he knew how. He'd failed Lewis and he'd never forgiven himself for that misstep.

And what about Annabelle? his brain demanded, reminding him that she had been grieving too. And he'd taken advantage of that, seeking solace in her arms, in her body, irrespective of the damage he might have been doing to her already tender heart.

'Annie Hargreaves is a long-time friend of the family,' he muttered, knowing it was the worst thing to say. It was feeding the flame with oxygen.

Ashton's laugh made Dimitrios want to snap something in half. 'A bit more than that, by the looks of it.'

Instincts took over, a ruthless streak turning his voice to stone. 'You do realise you're about to ruin a child's life for the sake of circulation?'

'And *you* claim to have a problem with that?'

Dimitrios couldn't respond. Zach and he had seen their world-wide viewership and readership treble in the last decade. He couldn't—wouldn't—trivialise the work journalists did.

He'd long since given up any hope that his life could be played out privately. Despite his personal wishes, he was considered to be someone of interest, a public figure, and his life—to some extent—was a free-for-all.

He ground his teeth together, the whole situation one that filled him with a sense of dark impatience.

'Let me get back to you.'

He hung up the phone and jammed it into his pocket, pushing away from the window without taking a step back from the glass.

'You must know how I feel about you, Dimitrios...'

'How you feel? Christ, Annabelle, you're little more than a child. I haven't thought about you or your feelings except for the fact you're Lewis's little sister.'

The little sister he'd promised Lewis he'd look after.

She'd winced.

'Then let me tell you now. I like you. I think I...no... I'm sure that I love you.'

It had been like having a gun pushed to his temple. Sheer panic flooded his nervous system. He'd made a mistake and it was going from bad to worse. He'd had to disabuse her of any idea that he could do this. He'd had to make a clean break, remove any hope she might have had that he could offer her more.

'You're deluding yourself. Nothing about this was "love". It was sex, plain and simple. And you know what the worst of it is? I was so drunk I barely even remember what we did.'

Her face had scrunched in pain and he'd been glad. He was pushing her away to punish himself—she *should* hate him. He deserved that.

'I have a life. A girlfriend.'

All the colour had drained from her face.

'And you are a mistake I'll always regret.'

Hell. Even now the words had the power to reach through time and make him feel a powerful sense of self-disgust. He'd done the right thing in pushing her away so forcefully, but seeing her heartbreak so clear on her face had made him feel like the worst kind of person. It was a feeling that had never really let up.

He crossed back to his desk, moving the mouse to stir his computer screen to life. The photograph was there, as large as it had been a moment ago, but it took on a whole new importance now.

He'd thought the boy looked familiar, but not in

a million years had he considered that he might be the father.

And Annabelle the mother.

Shock began to morph into something else.

Anger. Disappointment. Disbelief.

Why had she kept this from him?

'You'll always regret what we did? Well, I'll never forgive you for that. Just get out. Get out! Leave me alone. Don't ever contact me again.'

Had she been so angry she'd decided to keep their son from him? He'd wanted to push her away for good, but maybe he'd gone too far. Was this some sick form of payback? He couldn't believe it, yet the facts were there, staring right back at him. Annabelle had borne a child, and Dimitrios would bet his fortune on the fact he was the father.

Dimitrios ground his teeth together, his jaw set in a forbidding line as he reached for his desk phone and buzzed through to his hard-working assistant.

'Have the jet fuelled. I need to get to Sydney. Immediately.'

CHAPTER ONE

'THAT'S OKAY. I ate earlier.'

At six, Max was far too perceptive. His huge eyes lingered on Annie's face, as if studying her to see if it was true or not.

'I'm fine,' she assured him, curving her lips into a smile. 'Eat your dinner.'

He returned his attention to the plate in front of him, doing his best to hide the disappointment at the fact he was eating meatloaf for the third night in a row. He speared a piece with his fork, sliced it and lifted it. She watched him, her lips pursed.

'Are you working tonight, Mummy?'

She cast a glance at the laptop propped on the other end of the table. 'A little.'

He nodded, spearing another piece. Pleasure replaced worry. He was growing so fast, eating so much. It was just a growth spurt. He'd settle down soon enough. And hopefully the grocery bills wouldn't bankrupt her in the meantime.

She reached behind her and switched off the kitchen light, then took the seat beside Max, her hands curling around her mug of tea. The warmth was a balm.

'You can work now if you need to.'

Her heart turned over in her chest. 'I'd rather talk to you.'

'But then you'll have to stay up so late.'

She frowned. 'Why do you say that?'

He lifted his shoulders. 'You do, right?'

These last few nights she *had* been burning the candle at both ends. There'd been extra work to do in the firm and she'd put her hand up for it, glad of the additional hours. It wasn't the most highly paid work but the ability to do it from home meant she could be flexible for Max. When he'd been a baby, that had been imperative, but even now, with him at school, the number of holidays children took meant she needed to be able to care for him. There was no one who could help her—no nearby grandparents, aunts or uncles—and the cost of childcare was prohibitive.

'Sometimes. I like it, though. How's the meatloaf?' She winced at the conversation change— the last thing she wanted to do was remind him of the boring dinner he was being made to eat. She kept a bright smile pinned to her face, though. He matched it, nodded then reached for his drink.

He was so like his father.

Pain lanced her. She had to look away. Worry followed pain. A month ago, Max had asked about him. Not like when he'd been a younger boy and he'd become aware that children often had two parents. That had been an innocent, 'Do I have a daddy?' question that had been easy to palm off. This time, it had been laced with meaning. 'Who's my daddy, Mummy? Why haven't I met him? Does he live near us? Can I see him? Doesn't he love me?'

Difficult questions that had required thought and composure to answer. She'd always sworn she wouldn't lie to him, but answering his queries was a minefield.

Not for the first time, guilt at the way she was raising their child spread through her. Not just the relative poverty in which they lived, with Annie having to scrimp and save to afford even the most basic necessities, but the fact she was doing it alone.

A lump formed in her throat, the past heavy

in her mind. The night she'd gone to tell Dimitrios the truth had been one of the worst of her life. Seeing him three months after they'd slept together was something she'd had to brace herself for. She'd dressed in the most grown-up outfit she owned, hoping to look not just sexy and glamorous but mature as well, as though she belonged in his world with him. She'd had her speech all worked out—how he didn't need to be involved if he didn't want to be, but that he deserved to know.

But arriving to discover him surrounded by his exclusive, glamorous crowd in one of Sydney's most prestigious bars—and with the gorgeous redhead pressed to his body, all flame hair and milky skin—had sent Annie running. At eighteen, it had been too much to bear. Her pride had been hurt, her heart broken, and the precious kernel of meaning she'd taken from their night together had burst into flames, never to be recovered.

Lewis's death had left Annie completely alone. An already tenuous relationship with her parents had been irrevocably destroyed by their grief—an event that might have drawn them closer had pushed them apart, as Annie's mum refused to see that anyone else except her was hurting. Sleeping with Dimitrios had been the fulfilment of a long-cherished crush, but it had been more than that. Annie had been pulled out of the vortex of her pain and loneliness and put back together again in Dimitrios's arms. Being made love to by him had made her feel whole in a way she'd thought impossible, even if that pleasure was fleeting.

His words the next morning had robbed her of that sense of comfort, plunging her back into darkness and despair. She'd been eighteen and it had all been too much. Lewis's death, losing her virginity to Dimitrios and all that night had meant to her, his harsh rejection of her the next day, discovering she was pregnant and her mother's anger at that, the subsequent estrangement from her parents… Her emotions had been all over the place then but now, as a twenty-five-year-old, she wondered if she'd made the right decisions.

Was keeping Max from Dimitrios something she could still defend?

'What's wrong, Mummy?'

Whoops. She'd let her smile slip. She pushed

it back in place. 'Nothing, darling. Keep eating. It's late. You need to get to bed.'

Bedtime, though, had become something of a mission in the past six months. Gone were the days when Annie had been able to read a picture book, tuck the covers to Max's chin, kiss his forehead and slip from the room. It took an hour to settle him these days.

Tonight there was a story, answering a thousand and one questions, letting him have another sip of water, then a trip to the bathroom, then back to be tucked in again, then at least one call of, 'I'm scared, Mummy!'

At that point, Annie compromised and patted his back, even though all the parenting books seemed to suggest it was the wrong thing to do. At this point, it felt like the proverbial straw that was breaking the camel's back, anyway. She'd probably done so many little things wrong—what was one extra?

With a sigh, she crept from his room, pausing in the door frame to give his sleeping figure one last look. Love burst her heart. She was exhausted, worried and stressed but so full of love.

With a wistful smile, she clicked the door shut and moved back to the table. Her laptop beckoned. Cracking it open, she was glad of the distraction of work to keep her mind off the fact she was, actually, starving. She told herself she'd work for an hour and then have a cup of tea and an oat biscuit—her one indulgence. It wasn't usually so austere, but with Christmas just around the corner she needed to try to save enough to buy Max something. He did without so much for most of the year, while all his little friends were getting spoiled with books, sports equipment and anything their hearts desired. She wanted him to have *something* for Christmas.

Loading properties on to real-estate listings was work she could do without too much mental computation. She cross-checked the photographs with the property name and the description the various agents had attached, making sure each had uploaded correctly before moving on to the next.

Almost an hour after starting, a loud knock sounded at her door. She startled, quickly pushing her chair back. There was no worry that Max would stir—though he was difficult to get to sleep, once he was down for the night he slept like an immovable log. Nonetheless, the noise was loud and she needed to work.

It was probably a delivery for the flat upstairs. The house she lived in had been carved up by an industrious landlord many years earlier. Six small flats had been created and hers was the one at ground level; she often had deliveries intended for other residents simply because she was accessible.

'Just a second.' She closed the laptop and paused to flick on the kettle sitting on the peeling laminate bench top before unlocking the door. The peephole had been damaged years earlier and the landlord had never got round to replacing it, though at her insistence he'd added a chain lock. She slid it across now and opened the door as wide as the chain allowed.

Then had to fight every impulse she possessed to stop herself from pushing it shut again. Self-preservation and a thousand other impulses slammed into her.

Oh, damn.

Was it possible she'd somehow conjured him up? That her overactive mind and memories had willed him into her life again? What the hell was Dimitrios doing here?

She threw a guilt-laced look over her shoulder at her tiny, threadbare apartment.

'Annabelle.' His voice was like warm butter on brioche. He was one of the few people who used her full name. Her stomach clenched at memories of the way he'd said her name that night, of the way he'd touched her, the way he'd...

'I had half a bottle of whisky before coming here, Annabelle. Do you think I would ever have done this if I was in my right mind? I've never even looked at you before. You're just a kid, for God's sake. A teenager—and a naïve one at that. Don't mistake sex for anything of substance. This meant nothing.'

Recalling his words, and the hurt they'd inflicted, was exactly what she needed. She pulled herself to her full—admittedly not very impressive—height of five and a half feet and levelled him with what she hoped passed for an ice-cold glare. Inside, though, her heart was racing, making a mockery of any notion that she wasn't affected by him...

Max.

Their son.

He was asleep only a dozen metres or so away, behind a flimsy white wall. Panic surged through her.

'We have a problem.'

We. Just hearing him use that word sent a flood of warmth down her spine. It had been a long time since she'd been a 'we' with anyone except Max. The cold ache of loneliness was something with which Annie was completely familiar. She lifted one brow, unaware of the way his eyes followed the gesture, not noticing the frown that crossed his face.

'May I come in?'

She stared at him, belatedly realising she hadn't said anything to so much as acknowledge his presence. She was simply standing, staring, her heart in overdrive, her panic centres in full swing. She shook her head urgently, jerking it so hard it could well have snapped from her spine. 'Um, no. I— What are you doing here, Dimitrios?'

'That's something better discussed in private.'

She frowned. Beyond him was a Sydney cul-de-sac. No one was around, that she could see. 'Seems pretty private out there to me.' She reached for her key, hanging on a hook beside the door, then drew the door open further so she could step out.

She knew as she did so that it wasn't just the risk of him discovering the truth about Max. She was ashamed. Her apartment was far from luxurious—heck, it was far from *comfortable.* She'd done her best but there was always something more urgent to buy or pay for. Trendy cushions and throw rugs were way down her list of priorities.

Stepping outside, though, brought her toe-to-toe with a man she'd told herself she'd *never* see again. And even though she'd been coming to realise that was unrealistic—that their son deserved better—she hadn't been prepared for *this*! To see him tonight—here, at her place—was too much, too soon. She wasn't ready; she wasn't mentally prepared.

We have a problem.

'What are you doing here, Dimitrios?'

She registered the response her saying his name had on him. His eyes flickered with something she didn't comprehend. Annie looked away, crossing her arms over her chest. It had been a warm day, but the night had cooled off, and she was wearing only a thin T-shirt and yoga pants.

She'd almost forgotten how handsome he was. His face, so symmetrical, had the effect of having been sculpted from granite. Every line and shift was intentional—nothing had been left to chance. Cheekbones, a patrician nose, a determined jaw and a cleft in his chin that she remembered teasing with her tongue.

Her skin flushed with warmth. His eyes were a steely grey, blue in some lights, and his brows were flat and long, making him look every bit as intelligent as she knew him to be. She'd never known him without facial hair—stubble that grew over his chin and above his lip, but which she doubted was intentional, more the result of a man who was too busy to trouble himself with shaving regularly.

Her stomach lurched as other characteristics threw themselves into her mind. The memory of his hard chest, so chiselled and firm, each muscle drawing her attention and making her worship at the altar of his hyper-masculine beauty. His tan, a deep brown, the colour of burned caramel. His arms, strong and slim, the way they'd clamped around her and held her body close to his as she'd fallen asleep. And she'd fallen asleep believing the promises his body had made hers—that the experience they'd shared was the beginning of something meaningful and special. In the midst of her grief, the sadness that had filled her soul with the sudden death of her older brother, Annie had felt as though she'd come home. She'd believed everything would actually be okay.

'Why didn't you tell me?' He answered her question with one of his own. A *frisson* of danger moved down Annie's spine. The question wasn't the kind of thing you asked. This was no fishing expedition; he knew something. Or, he *thought* he knew something. But what? Hopefully, she racked her brain for anything else it could be—hopefully. But there was nothing. The only secret she'd ever kept from him—from anyone—was the existence of Max.

Anxiety turned to adrenaline; she shivered.

'Tell you what?' she heard herself ask, her voice a little higher in pitch than normal.

'It's too late for that, Annabelle.' He expelled a breath that could almost have passed for a sigh except there was too much anger behind it; bitterness, too. 'A journalist knows. We have a son together.'

She sucked in a sharp breath, pressing her back against the door in an effort to stay upright. It barely helped. She felt as though the four walls were closing in on her—as though the atmosphere of the planet was being sucked out into space, as though an enormous weight was bearing down hard on her belly.

Why had she thought she could get away with this? Of course he should have known about Max. What had she been thinking?

All the reasons that had seemed so valid a little over six years ago blew away from her like dust in the wind. She stared at him, but the accusation and anger in his face made it impossible to hold his gaze for long. She angled her face away, concentrating on breathing. Her lungs burned. Shame made her cheeks flame.

Her eyes hurt.

A second later, she was aware of his curse, and then nothing. She wasn't sure how long the nothingness lasted, only that his hands were around her waist, lifting her easily as his fingers dug into her pocket to remove her keys. She was groggy—too shocked to protest. He pushed open the door to her apartment and it wasn't within her capability to feel even a hint of embarrassment in that moment—at least, not at her décor.

He carried her to the sofa and laid her down, his footsteps retreating for a moment. She heard squeaking as he opened cupboards and then slamming as they closed heavily. Once, twice, thrice, a fourth time, and then the running of water. He returned with a glass and held it out to her. 'Drink this.'

God, what she must look like to him! She scrambled into a sitting position, holding a shaking hand out for the glass. After she'd had half of it, she sat with it cradled in her lap, fighting the sting of tears.

'So it's true?'

She lifted her face to his, wishing he would sit down or that she could stand up, but her knees were as stable as jelly. And, given the tiny size of her sofa, she didn't actually want him to sit down, because that would bring him way too close to her, and she was already spiralling from the remembered sensation of his strong arms carrying her so easily when she'd passed out.

His voice was throaty and deep, raw and guttural. 'Annabelle, damn it. Tell me. Is it true?'

Except he didn't really doubt the truth, did he? She saw that in his expression, the tautness of his face, the anger in the depths of his eyes. Her stomach squeezed. She couldn't lie to him—not any more. And she didn't *want* to. Nor did she want to lie to Max.

But, oh, Max. How would she explain this to

him? She knotted her fingers in her lap, an old nervous habit she'd never been able to shed, her eyes huge in a face that had grown pale. Her side-sweeping fringe had fallen to cover one of her eyes in a river of shimmering gold and she instinctively lifted a hand to swipe at it, tucking the longer strands behind her ear.

She hadn't really thought she could keep Dimitrios from learning the truth. But it was only having him here, with this accusation, that she realised she'd waited for this day—that she'd known it was coming and had almost longed for it. What else could explain the relief she felt?

He knew. Finally.

It was over.

No more secrets and lies—at least, not to Max. 'Yes.'

He flinched, his cheeks darkening. Perhaps she'd been wrong about him; maybe he hadn't already known? His jaw tightened, as though he was grinding his teeth together. She looked down at her knees because she couldn't bear to look at him a moment longer. 'He's six and his name is Max. I have photos—'

'Photos?' His voice made thick with emotion.

'Give me one reason why I shouldn't go into his room right now and take him away with me!'

Her heart skipped several beats; her lungs failed to inflate. She reached for the arm of the sofa in shock, gripping it hard, feeling as though her eyes were filling with darkness again. She stood up quickly, shaky legs or not, needing to feel more physically prepared for that kind of challenge.

'I've already seen a photo. The journalist had one.'

That stopped Annie in her tracks. Despite the shock, her rational brain began to assert itself. He'd mentioned a journalist earlier, only she'd been so blindsided by seeing him here she hadn't registered that point. 'What journalist?'

'Does it matter?'

'No one can know about this. It's impossible.'

Dimitrios's eyes narrowed. 'You made sure of that?'

She swallowed, hearing the silver blade to his voice, the undercurrent of displeasure that he had every right to feel. 'Yes.' She had; she was sure of it.

'Not well enough, apparently.'

'It's just not possible.' She shook her head. 'He

doesn't share your surname. No one ever knew about…' She stumbled, biting down on her lip, as the traitorous word 'us' had been about to escape. There had never been an 'us'. That implied togetherness. Friendship. A relationship, even. They'd had an ill-thought-out one-night stand. Nothing more meaningful than that. 'What happened that night,' she finished awkwardly.

'You never mentioned it to anyone?' he pushed, and his obvious doubts on that score raised her feminist hackles.

'What's the matter, Dimitrios? Does that hurt your pride? Did you think I would scream what we'd done from the rooftops?'

A muscle jerked in his jaw and she had a sense he was trying very hard not to give into his anger. Only she found she *wanted* his anger—it felt appropriate, given what they'd been through and were now discussing.

He spoke calmly, but she could see how that cost him. 'I thought you were a decent person; I believed you to be like Lewis.' She recoiled at the invocation of her brother's name, at Dimitrios using Lewis against her like that. 'But a decent person would never have kept something like this from me.'

'A decent person wouldn't have said all the things you did to me that night,' she responded in kind, carefully keeping her voice soft, though it shook with the effort. 'A decent person wouldn't have shown up drunk on my doorstep—days after my brother's funeral, might I add—and spent the night making love to me only to throw in my face the next morning how little that—*I*—meant to you.'

His expression was inscrutable, but his body was wound tighter than a coil. 'And so this is retaliation? You wanted to hurt me?'

She shook her head. 'No, never.' Her reaction was instant. 'It wasn't about that.'

Silence fell, barbed. No, not silence. There was breathing: heavy, fast…his, hers…it filled the room like a tornado of emotions.

'You told me you would forget about me in days, do you remember that?'

Somehow, the only shift in his features was a tightening about his mouth.

'You told me you were so drunk I could have been any woman—you'd found your way to my door but that was just happenstance.'

'You don't need to repeat what I said. I remember.'

Something sharp moved in the region of her heart. She was glad he remembered.

'You told me you had a girlfriend,' she reminded him anyway, her hands on her hips, her chin jutting forward. She'd hated him then, for taking what had been an incredible night for her—her first sexual experience with a man she'd already been halfway to loving, the comfort and sense of unity she'd felt—and turning it into something so tawdry and *wrong*. She would *never* have slept with him if she'd known he was with someone else!

'Yes.' No apology, yet she saw something stir in the depths of his eyes, something she didn't understand and didn't want to waste time analysing.

'All of which makes me a bastard of the first order,' he said firmly. 'But that still doesn't excuse you hiding our son from me for six damn years.'

She spun away from him, moving to the window that overlooked the street. She'd tried to tell him. She hadn't wanted to do it this way. But seeing him, his lifestyle, how could she throw something like a child into the midst of that? She'd been terrified. What if he'd sued for custody?

And raised her child with another woman? She'd already lost so much—her parents, Lewis—the prospect of their baby was all she had.

Seeing him in his own environment like that had shown her the impossibility of telling him *anything,* and the words he'd thrown at her had been like flames, licking at her feet, tormenting her with how little she meant to him. Why would she ever have believed Dimitrios would act in her best interests? She meant nothing to him—he would do as he wanted, irrespective of her wishes.

Convinced of that, she'd fled, and all these years she'd told herself he'd be grateful if he ever learned the truth.

'How did the journalist find out?' she asked quietly, returning to her original question, her face creased with concentration.

'Beats me. Apparently you must have told someone.'

She shook her head. 'I have no idea how a journalist could have discovered this. I've been so careful.'

'And what about my son? Does he know?'

My son. So possessive, so…right. For years she'd thought of Max as *hers.* He was her child, hers to protect, raise, love and shepherd. Except, the older he'd got, the more he'd started to look like Dimitrios, so that it was becoming impossible to ignore his true parentage.

'He doesn't know.'

Dimitrios's response was a rumble, a curse, a moan, low and quiet. It nonetheless reverberated around the room and pressed deep from his soul and into Annie's. She winced, his pain impossible to miss.

'You haven't even told him about me?'

She shook her head softly. 'He's started to ask, though. I've known for a while that I would need to...'

'And would you then have told me, also?'

She turned back to face him, wishing she could lie, but knowing he finally deserved the truth. 'I don't know.' It was the best she could do. 'I'd like to believe so.'

His eyes bore into hers, as though through the power of sight he could somehow intuit the truth of her heart. Her blood moved like wildfire and the hairs on her arms stood up.

She waited for him to say something, to react, but he stood there for so long her blood began to rush for another reason altogether. She stared at him. A cacophony of emotions filled her, so she took a small step backwards, needing to break the connection that was firing between them like an electrical current. How was it possible that even in this moment he could have any kind of impact on her?

'I—' She wasn't sure what she'd intended to say. She stopped talking when he shook his head and held up a hand, as if to silence her.

'No.' His brows drew closer. 'No,' he repeated, then turned on one heel and took the five or so steps his long gait needed to get him to the door.

'You're leaving?' she demanded.

At the door, he turned to face her. 'I won't do this now.'

Her jaw dropped.

'If you knew how close I was to saying a thousand things I would come to regret, then you'd understand.' He shook his head. 'If I've learned anything, it's to not react when your emotions are in play.'

She stared at him in disbelief.

'I will come back tomorrow.'

She swallowed. 'Max has school.'

'Good. We should talk without him hearing—it will be easier to make plans if he's not present.'

'Plans for what?' But she already knew what he was going to say. Custody. He was going to take Max away, at least some of the time. How could she live with that? Panic filled her. She felt as if she might vomit.

'For our marriage, Annabelle. What else?'

CHAPTER TWO

SHE COULD HARDLY turn a sow's ear into a silk purse but she'd done the best she could, polishing and tidying, neatening the small apartment to within an inch of its life in preparation for Dimitrios's return. Her whole world felt completely tipped off-balance.

For our marriage, Annabelle. What else?

As though it were a *fait accompli*—a given.

It was *so* like Dimitrios. He was born to command, a Titan of any boardroom he entered, a man people couldn't help but respond to and obey. Naturally it wouldn't have occurred to him that she might not wish to be married to him.

But...hello!

How in the world could he possibly think she'd go along with this? They hadn't seen each other in seven years, and that had been a spectacular disaster. She was still sifting through the shrapnel of that evening, let alone the emotional fallout that had come after.

After he'd left.

After she'd found out she was pregnant.

After she'd gone to tell him.

After she'd seen him with his girlfriend, surrounded by people like him.

After she'd had their baby.

She felt as though she'd boarded some kind of express train and hadn't been able to pause to draw breath. Marriage? Impossible.

Knots tangled inside her belly.

She moved to the kitchen and wiped the counters for the third time that morning, then pressed the button on the kettle, exhaling slowly as she did so. It was grey outside, gloomy and hot, the kind of late-spring day that typified the tropics. The clouds sat low in the sky, thick like a blanket, holding Sydney hostage to humidity and the lure of rain—a relief that wouldn't come.

Annie caught her reflection in the window, darkened from the outside, and winced. Having seen the kind of women he associated with, she understood why his rejection of her had been so fierce that night.

How could a man like Dimitrios Papandreo ever really be interested in her? She'd dressed with care that morning, pulling on her best pair of jeans and a neat, white linen blouse she'd found in a charity shop about a month earlier. She'd pulled her silky blonde hair into a pony tail, then yanked it straight back out again and brushed it until it shone, before deciding the pony tail was best after all. She'd run through the process a few more times before giving up in frustration and allowing it to fall around her shoulders, unintentionally creating the impression of a golden halo.

She didn't generally wear cosmetics unless she was going somewhere for work—which was very rare—and she didn't really own very much in the way of make-up. But as a concession to their meeting, and out of a desire to feel her very best, she'd dashed some pale-pink lipstick across her mouth and dabbed a bit to the apples of her cheeks, blending it until it just gave a hint of much-needed colour to her pale skin. Her nails were short, her feet bare, and there wasn't much she could do about the expression of worry that had taken up residence on her features.

The kettle clicked off; she reached for a tea cup on autopilot, placing it on the bench top, adding a herbal bag and filling it with water. She stared at the swirling waves of steam, trying not to contemplate how completely her life was about to change. One way or another—marriage or not—nothing would ever be the same again.

She'd just taken a sip of her tea when the doorbell rang. Startled, she moved abruptly, spilling a gush of boiling liquid over her shirt. She swore, pulling the shirt from her skin, wincing at the hint of pain and shaking her head at her own clumsiness, before moving in the direction of the door.

She wrenched it open, barely giving Dimitrios more than a passing glance—nonetheless, it was enough to send her pulse into overdrive. 'Come in. Have a seat. I'll just be a second.' She moved down the tiny hallway and into the room she was using as her own—it had been designed as a study, a small adjunct to the single bedroom, but it worked better for Max to have the bedroom. While he didn't have many toys, those he did have were very precious to him. She liked him to have space to play with the train tracks he'd been collecting, as well as the books he brought home from the library.

She pulled a replacement from her wardrobe, a simple yellow T-shirt, and changed quickly. The skin above her breasts was pink from where the water had landed but it didn't hurt. Sparing a brief second to check her appearance before she left the room, she almost instantly turned away again, hating to think about the ways she'd changed since that night.

At eighteen she'd been youthful and, despite the grief following Lewis's death, she'd been full of brightness and spark. Her future had all been ahead of her—choices to be made, a university degree to be attained. She looked far older than her twenty-five years, Annie thought with a frown. She didn't see the way the light picked up the colours of her eyes—sparks of blue alongside silver and green. Nor did she see the way the sunshine-yellow shirt complemented her deep brown tan, or the way her slender frame hadn't lost the curves of her breasts and hips.

When she emerged a moment later into the stillness of her living area, it was to see Dimitrios had overtaken the space completely. Not with anything he was doing, just by the simple act of being there. He was big—large—his frame too much for the room, his presence too dynamic and demanding. Annie worked alone, and sometimes a whole day could pass in which she wouldn't hear another human's voice. Everything about her life was small, quiet and unremarkable. Dimitrios was like a blade of lightning splitting that apart.

'I spilled something on my shirt,' she said quietly, self-conscious about her apartment. He was dressed in a suit that, she would bet her non-existent savings, had cost more than her year's rent. Slate-grey with a light blue shirt, it was clearly hand-made and tailored to his frame.

He nodded once, a crisp movement of his head, and gestured towards the table. 'Shall we get down to business?'

Despite the tension, a smile tightened her lips. Just as she remembered. All command, completely in charge. Well, that didn't hurt. For now, she could let him call the shots. Besides, she was curious to hear just what he was suggesting, even when she had no intention of accepting his ludicrous proposal.

'Of course. I've just made a tea. Would you like something?'

'No, this won't take long.'

How romantic. She bit back the sarcastic rejoinder. She didn't want—nor expect—romance from Dimitrios. It was no surprise he wasn't even pretending to offer it. In a small act of defiance, she moved into the kitchen and grabbed her own tea cup, taking a moment to replenish it with boiling water. She was conscious of his eyes on her the whole time, watching as she added more water and returned the original tea bag to the cup, using a spoon to hasten its brewing and to capture all the flavour she could from the single bag.

When she moved to the table, his eyes followed her, and as she sat down she looked at him properly, catching the frown on his face. No surprises there. He was probably wondering how to politely extricate himself from the parting statement he'd made the night before.

Politely? Who was she kidding? This was Dimitrios Papandreo. Having been on the receiving end of his barbed tongue, there was no need to expect kindness from him. Reminding herself of that, she straightened her spine, regarding him with icy patience.

'Well, Dimitrios?' she prompted, cradling her hands around the tea. 'What would you like to discuss?'

It seemed to jerk him out of his reverie. He nodded, reaching into his pocket and pulling out some sheets of folded paper. The table wasn't large—it could seat four at a pinch. He extended his arm a little, holding the papers to her. 'I've had a pre-nuptial agreement drawn up. Nothing complicated.' He looked around the apartment. 'I presume you don't have a lot of assets, but whatever you do have will of course be quarantined from me, for you to retain in your name only.'

She didn't make any effort to take the papers. She was blindsided that instead of attempting to back-pedal on his marriage proposal he was instead doubling down.

'Naturally, the terms are generous towards you. As for our son, he will inherit what you would expect, as well as have access to a trust fund incrementally—on his eighteenth birthday, his twenty-first and his twenty-fifth.' Perhaps mistaking her silence for gratitude or acquiescence, he paused a moment then continued. 'It's as it was for Zach and me, and for my father. It works well. Better than receiving an enormous amount at eighteen, when you're more interested in alcohol and women than being sensible with investments.'

Annie felt as if a rock had landed at the base of her throat. She couldn't swallow properly; her tongue wouldn't cooperate. She sipped her tea, which helped only a little.

'As for where we'll live, I'm not sure if you're aware, but I relocated to Singapore about four years ago. My house is more than adequate for you and our son and any other children—'

She spluttered, her butter-yellow shirt very nearly another casualty of the tea. 'Hold on.' She took a sip, then deliberately replaced the cup on the edge of the table, her fingertips shaking as the reality of what he was suggesting—and the fact he was clearly serious—overtook her.

'I'm not marrying you, Dimitrios, so please stop making plans as though any of this is actually happening.'

He didn't react. She realised then that he'd been expecting some opposition.

'The amount of your allowance is, of course, negotiable.'

She flicked her gaze to the piece of paper he held, then shook her head. 'There's no price on my head. You can't buy me.'

'No?' His teeth were bared in a smile, but it was born of anger. 'I disagree.'

She stayed where she was even as she felt as though bees were flying into her. 'I'm not mercenary. Not even a little. Don't you think that, if money had been any kind of factor for me, I would have contacted you well before this? Do you have any idea how hard these last seven years have been for me? How I've struggled and sacrificed, all for our son? Who, by the way, is called Max. And don't even get me started on how offensive I find it that you've been here ten minutes and haven't asked me one single thing about him.'

A muscle jerked in Dimitrios's jaw and his eyes stirred with unmistakable anger. 'Do you think I want to hear about my own son from you? No, Annabelle. I want to get to know him, but for myself, not through your eyes. He's my child, and I should have been a part of his life well before now.'

The rebuke was like a blade sliding beneath her rib cage, because he was right. She ignored that, though.

'I see how you've been living, how you've been raising my son. Do you think any of this—' he gestured around the room '—is good enough?'

Hurt simmered in her blood. She swept her eyes shut, so didn't see the way he frowned and pushed back in his seat a little, shaking his head in frustration.

'No.' It was just a whisper. 'But I've been doing my best. So don't come in here and insult me, because I won't have it, Dimitrios. You have no idea what this has been like—'

'And whose fault is that?'

She pressed her lips together, sadness flooding her.

'I can't change the past. If you want to be a part of Max's life, I understand, but there's no way we can just pick up and move to Singapore, nor that I would ever marry you. This isn't the nineteenth-century. There's no morality police set to charge you for having a kid out of wedlock, or whatever.'

'There are my morals,' he said simply. 'And there is my son's future.'

'Your morals are your problem, not mine. And as for Max's future—' she inserted his name with determination '—that's something we can discuss.'

'I'm more than happy to discuss the minor details of our situation, but not the solution. We are getting married, Annabelle, so stop fighting me and start getting used to it.' He leaned closer, bracing his elbows on the table. 'Start preparing for it—be happy. All of your worries will be gone from the minute you become my wife.'

A shiver ran down her spine and instinctively she rejected that. All her worries would just be beginning if she became his wife—why couldn't he see that?

'Why are you being so insistent about this? You seem to have had a string of glamorous, high-profile girlfriends, and you've never married any of them, so I can only presume you feel as disinterested in being someone's husband as I do in being your wife.'

'It's true, marriage has never been on my agenda.'

'Never?'

He held her gaze a long time. 'No.'

'Then why now?'

'Max is a game-changer.'

Max is a game-changer. How true that was! For her, it had been a complete game-changer in every way. No university. No shiny, bright career. No friends—it had been too hard to keep up with them with a small baby at home.

'Max is your son,' she agreed quietly. 'But that has nothing to do with you and me—we can both be a part of his life without having to be a part of each other's.'

'That's not good enough.'

'None of this is good enough,' she agreed with quiet insistence. 'But it's the card we've been dealt.'

He held her gaze for several beats. 'I've organised a town-hall wedding. It's better if we marry quietly, then deal with the fall-out and the press later.'

Annie had the strangest sensation that she was speaking a foreign language.

'The...fall-out? Press? I'm *not* marrying you.' She paused after each word in the last sentence for emphasis, and because she couldn't wrap her tongue around the sounds properly.

'If you would like to have a bigger wedding, we can arrange that in due course. I'll leave those arrangements up to you. As for your life in Singapore, are you working at the moment?'

She stared at him, a frown drawing her brows together, forming a crease between them. It was all so absurd that she found herself answering anyway. 'I— Yes. I have a job.'

'What do you do?'

Her frown deepened. 'I load properties on to

real-estate websites. I work for several agencies.' She bit down on her lip. 'It's something I can do from home, so when Max was little it made a lot of sense. Now he's at school, but with the holidays and the short days, and the possibility he might be sick and I need time off, the job still suits me.'

Dimitrios's expression was inscrutable. 'What happened to university?'

A wave of nostalgia passed through her. Not sadness, exactly, because she could never be sad about Max's arrival, even when it had signalled the end of so many of her dreams. No, it was nostalgia for the young woman she'd once been.

'Max happened,' she reminded him. 'I couldn't exactly have a baby and complete a law degree.'

He leaned forward, interlocking his fingers and placing his hands between them. 'You were accepted on to a top course, if I remember…'

She wouldn't allow herself to feel even a hint of warmth at his recollection. Dimitrios was a details man. He'd filed the titbit of biographical information for no reason other than it was what he did.

'It wasn't feasible.'

'Your parents?'

'They moved to Perth.'

His brow lifted. 'When?'

'After Lewis died.' She swallowed hard, the pain of that still difficult to process. Annie had learned then that nothing was stable, or permanent. She'd lost her brother and to all intents and purposes her parents in the space of a few months. Life was a rollercoaster with zero guarantees. 'Mum found it too hard to stay here. Everywhere reminded her of him. She needed a fresh start.'

'You were only eighteen, and you were pregnant. Why didn't you go with them?'

'We never had a great relationship.' She was uncertain why she was confiding in him. 'They weren't awful to us or anything when Lewis and I were growing up, but they fought a lot, and it was tense. I think Mum wanted everything to be different for me. Finding out I'd got pregnant and planned to raise a baby on my own, that I'd never go to university and my future was "over"—as she said—made her furious. She wanted me to put Max up for adoption.'

Dimitrios's face was like a thundercloud. 'You're not serious? Rather than offer to help you?'

Annie shrugged. 'It was a no-brainer. They

moved to Perth, I stayed here and had Max. Over time, they've mellowed. They love him. I tolerate them for that reason alone.'

Her smile was bittersweet. 'Besides, everything reminded me of Lewis here too. Unlike Mum, I didn't want to run from those memories. Sometimes I find myself going past his old place, just letting that wash over me—how happy he was the day he moved in, how much he loved his life.' She shook her head sadly. 'I didn't feel like I could leave that—him. Sydney is a connection to him. I suppose that sounds silly.'

Dimitrios's voice was husky when he spoke. 'Not at all. I get it.'

'Do you?'

He nodded once and something dangerous passed between them because it was so reminiscent of their shared grief—a guttural, exhaustive sadness that had drawn them together that night. She looked away, focussing on the wall opposite. Scuff marks she'd become used to now seemed so much darker and worse. Embarrassment filled her but she refused to surrender to it.

His tone softened, sympathy obvious. 'I have an apartment here. We can travel back often. I don't intend to uproot you from your life completely.'

She shook her head. 'You're not hearing me. Marriage isn't the solution here.'

He didn't answer that.

'Why did you call him Max?'

Annie's cheeks burned pink. The sentimentality filled her with shame. She wouldn't tell him the truth—it was too much of a concession, and she wasn't ready to give him so much. Admitting that she'd researched his family tree and chosen his grandfather's name somehow made her feel vulnerable, like the silly eighteen-year-old she'd been, the one who'd cared too much. 'I heard the name and liked it,' she said simply.

'I like it too.'

Silence fell, thick with feeling.

'You can come back to Sydney any time you'd like,' he said with a gentleness that threatened to bring tears to her eyes. 'I understand how this city holds a connection to Lewis for you.' He paused. 'It does for me too.'

Their eyes met and something like mutual understanding weaved from him to her, binding them in an inexplicable way, just as it had that night.

'Max can still come and see his friends. But, for the most part, your lives will be in Singapore. There's an international school he can attend—it's very good.'

But Annie was shaking her head again, refusing to succumb to the image he was painting. 'What part of "no" don't you understand? I can't marry you.'

'Why not?'

The question surprised her, her inability to answer even more so. She searched for something that made sense, something that would satisfy him, and drew a blank.

'Because' or 'I just can't' didn't feel sufficient.

'What? Do you have a lover? A boyfriend?'

Her cheeks flamed. No way would Annie confess the mortifying truth to Dimitrios—that she'd been alone since that one night they'd shared, seven years earlier!

'Marriage just…isn't something you decide to do on the spur of the moment.'

'Even when a child is involved?' he prompted, gently cajoling.

'Especially when there's a child involved!' Her reply was emphatic, born of personal experience.

'Neither of us wants to subject Max to that kind of marriage.'

'What kind of marriage, exactly?'

She pursed her lips, pushing away memories of her childhood. Memories of her parents, who'd fought constantly, who'd been so out of sync, always worried about money, quarrelling with each other, and, when they weren't together, shouting at their children. 'One where we argue and snap. I don't want Max to think that's what family life is all about.'

'I don't intend to argue with you once we're married.'

'So what do you intend once we're married?'

The question appeared to unsettle him for a moment.

Feeling she'd claimed the sensible high ground, she pushed home her advantage. 'You can't actually picture this, can you, Dimitrios? You and me, husband and wife, for as long as we both shall live?'

His eyes were swirling with the intensity of his thoughts.

'Or is this just an arrangement until Max is a bit older? Twelve? Fifteen? Eighteen? At what point do you imagine we'll walk away from this farce you're proposing and get on with our real lives?'

His Adam's apple jerked as he swallowed. 'I promised Lewis I would look after you.'

Annie had to reach behind her for some form of support. 'What?' The word was just a croak.

Dimitrios's expression was grim. 'Before he died.' He looked distinctly uncomfortable—rife with grief. 'He was worried about you. Your parents, the way they treated you…' He shook his head. 'He asked me to keep an eye on you.'

Annie stared at him for several anguished seconds, tears thick in her throat. It was so like Lewis; oh, how she missed her big brother! 'I didn't know.'

'No.' He grimaced. 'Well, I didn't exactly follow through on what I'd promised him.' She understood then—he felt guilty, just as she did, but his guilt had nothing to do with the awful things he'd said to her, the way he'd rejected her so cruelly. No, his guilt was because he'd betrayed Lewis and the promise he'd made. It didn't make her feel better, but it did make a sad kind of sense of what had happened back then.

'That's why you came to me that night? To check up on me?'

He didn't answer. He didn't need to. It shone a new light on how one-sided their passion had been.

'I promised him I'd take care of you, and I've badly neglected that promise. I had no idea how badly until recently but, Annabelle, I intend to fix this. I intend to look after you.'

Her heart twisted, pride snapping inside her. 'And if I don't want looking after? If I point out that I can do that all for myself?'

He leaned closer and her body tightened in an unwelcome response. 'I can't tell you what our marriage will be like. I'm acting on instinct here, and every instinct is telling me getting married is the only thing that makes sense. I promise you this, though—I will never neglect your needs again, Annabelle.'

She ground her teeth together, knowing the importance of fighting him. 'Stop speaking as though this is going to happen.'

'But it is going to happen.'

'You do realise this is the twenty-first century? And that I'm a woman with my own ability to make this decision?'

'The decision has been taken out of our hands.'

'Why do you say that?'

He pushed back in his chair, regarding her with eyes that were impossible to read. 'What do you know of my life?'

The question was unexpected. 'Not a lot,' she admitted.

'You know my family is wealthy.'

She rolled her eyes. 'You're a Papandreo. Your family isn't just "wealthy". You're richer than Croesus. What's your point?'

'That money brings with it a mountain of consequences.'

'Like never having to work a day in your life?'

He arched a brow. She regretted the waspish comment as soon as she'd said it. Both Zach and Dimitrios worked harder than just about anyone. Casting aspersions on their dedication was just petty. 'I'm sorry. I didn't mean that.' She sighed. 'For the record, that's exactly the kind of snappy comment I don't want Max growing up having to hear.'

His grin melted something deep inside her, filling her with warmth. 'So don't snap at me, then.'

'Easier said than done,' she muttered, taking another sip of her tea.

'From the minute my brother and I went to live

with our father, there has been press intrusion in our lives. Paparazzi, ridiculous stories, speculative documentaries asserting all sorts of fanciful "truths".' He shook his head scathingly. 'While we have become used to that nonsense, you're not. Max isn't.' He leaned closer again, and his masculine fragrance tickled her nostrils, causing her gut to clench in powerful response. 'There is no question of keeping this a secret. A reporter *knows*. This story will break soon, and your life will change in ways you can't anticipate. I can't protect you here. I can't protect you unless you're in my home, living with me. I can't protect Max unless he's in my house, where I can see him. Don't you get that?'

She gulped, the reality of what he was saying banging into her hard.

'I—can cope with reporters,' she mumbled not at all convincingly, to either of them. 'I mean, I'll learn to cope.'

'Perhaps. But in the meantime you'll expose Max to unnecessary difficulties and drama, all because you won't be reasonable.'

'Reasonable?' Her jaw dropped. 'Marrying you is the opposite of reasonable! It's preposterous. I haven't seen you in seven years and the last time I did see you was—hardly a success,' she pointed out, shaking her head, then closing her eyes against the deluge of memories threatening to weaken her.

'This isn't about us any more.' His voice rang with certainty. 'Max is my number-one priority.'

'You haven't even met him.'

Dimitrios's expression barely shifted, yet a shiver ran down Annie's spine. 'A point I wouldn't labour, if I were you.'

She bit down on her lip. 'I only meant that he's also my number-one priority. Don't swoop in and act as if you're the only one capable of prioritising him.'

'With all due respect, Annabelle, when I look around this home I see someone who is proud— to a fault. You described me a moment ago as "richer than Croesus", and yet you have been living here in abject poverty, barely making ends meet.'

'That's presumptuous of you.'

'No, it's not. Your credit rating is in dire straits, you're weeks behind in the paltry rental payments, you don't have private health insurance, you don't have a car, you look as though you haven't eaten in a week...'

She gasped. 'Dimitrios…have you had me investigated?'

'You kept my child from me. Don't you think I had a right to find out how he's been living?'

Annie tried to calm her racing heart but she felt as though she were drowning in the sea of his accusations.

'You could have just asked me.'

His eyes held a silent challenge. He didn't need to say what he was thinking—she could read it in his face. *You might have lied.* Inexplicably, tears filled her eyes. She blinked rapidly to clear them, but one escaped and slid slowly down her cheek, dripping on to the table top.

'This is not the end of the world.' His words were gentle.

She stood uneasily, running a hand through her hair as she moved into the kitchen. She wasn't particularly thirsty but restlessness made her act. She pulled two glasses down and filled them from the tap, before returning to the table.

'I can't imagine how you must feel,' she said softly, shaking her head. 'You're being so calm and reasonable, but you must feel…'

His eyes sparked with hers for a moment and her heart turned over in her chest.

'Yes, I feel,' he agreed gruffly. 'I have missed six years of our son's life—because of a decision you made.' He mirrored her earlier gesture, pushing his chair back and standing, crossing his arms. 'I feel everything you might expect,' he said, his voice lowering, calming, his eyes showing anguish but not anger. 'But what good can come of making you pay for that now?'

His eyes probed hers for several long seconds, as though he was scanning her innermost thoughts, assessing her piece by piece.

'Should I punish you, Annabelle? Take our child away from you, like you took him away from me?'

A shiver ran the length of her spine and she lifted a hand, pressing it over her mouth.

'Should I put you through a legal battle you definitely cannot afford, and which I will undoubtedly win? Should I make sure the press has all the gory details, so that you're branded all over the Internet as the kind of woman who'd keep a child separated from his father?'

She wrapped her arms around her slender frame, her eyes huge in her delicate face.

'Don't think these options didn't occur to me. I left last night because each and every one of them was running through my mind, begging to be thrown at you, hurled in a way that could cause the most damage. Surely you deserve that?'

Pain tore through her.

'But then I thought of the little boy, and how much he must love you. I thought of how, when he is a man, he will judge me for the decisions I make today. He will look at me as a hero or a villain based on how I treat you—his mother. And so I came here to extend an olive branch I'm not sure you deserve, but that I need you to accept. Because I will do whatever it takes to have him in my life.'

It was too much. Too kind, too reasonable, so full of love for their child—not his, not hers but theirs. Yet there was still the lurking undertone of a threat. She could tell he didn't want to carry his threats out, yet he would. Of course he would! If she didn't comply, he would take Max away from her.

She couldn't let that happen, even when the idea of marrying Dimitrios terrified her.

'Marriage is—' She hesitated, thinking of all the childish fairy-tales Lewis had filled her head with. 'It's meant to be so much more than this.'

A muscle jerked in his jaw. 'Meaning?'

'It's meant to be about love,' she whispered. And, while she felt stupid and naïve, it was also important for her to admit her belief in that. He was asking her to go against everything she knew to be true.

'For some people it is,' he agreed. 'But for others, it's a convenient arrangement. All marriages are an exchange. Ours won't be based on love but that doesn't mean it can't still be good—for both of us.'

Her heart cracked. Not once had Lewis told her about something so pragmatic. She felt a chasm forming inside her, the reality of her situation clear—the rightness of what he was proposing and the reasons she should agree. But the belief she'd always carried in her heart—that one day she'd be swept off her feet by Prince Charming—was smouldering into ashes.

'I need to think about it,' she said quietly. 'Is that okay?'

His eyes held hers for several seconds, each making her heart twist and her pulse throb, but finally he nodded—just once, a shift of his head, a turn of his body. He began to walk; she waited for him to go past her, but as he reached her he stopped, staring down into her eyes, his expression one she couldn't understand.

'Think fast, Annabelle. I've waited six years. I won't wait much longer to be his father.'

'Yes. He's my son.' Dimitrios's tone gave little away. The admission was already more than he ideally wanted to concede, yet using the press to his advantage made sense, given the circumstances. If Annabelle wanted time to think, then she should at least see the full picture. At the moment, the idea of media intrusion was simply hypothetical to her.

'No kidding.' Ashton's laugh was unpalatable. 'Six years old?'

'Yes.'

'And was I right about the mother?'

It was a turning point. Once he confirmed her name, there would be no going back. 'Yes. Annabelle Hargreaves.'

'How did you meet her?'

Dimitrios's lip curled in contempt. 'You're going to have to do some of the leg work yourself. If you want to invade my privacy, I can't stop you, but I'm not going to spoon-feed you the story.'

Another laugh. 'Have you got a statement for me, then?'

He narrowed his eyes, aware that he was crossing a line he couldn't uncross. He thought of their son and leaned forward, knowing he really had no choice. Just as Annabelle didn't. From the moment they'd conceived this child, their futures had been sealed. 'Annabelle and I have known each other a long time. Recently, we rekindled our romance. We were taking it slowly—for our son's sake—but now I'm happy for the world to know. We're getting married—as soon as it can be arranged.'

CHAPTER THREE

THE FLASH EXPLODED in her face like lightning striking. Annie startled, instinctively pulling her hat down lower. There were at least a dozen photographers standing on the footpath, all shouting questions at her. It was hard to discern a single one from the eruption of voices.

'How did you keep the billionaire's love child a secret for so long?'

'Is it true he's never met his father?'

'What are you wearing to the wedding?'

'Can we see the ring?'

'Have you been seeing him all this time?'

'How have you put up with the other women?'

'Is it true there are twins as well?'

Aghast, she kept her head lowered and moved quickly, but they followed behind, hounding Annie as she walked, shouting questions. When she was only a block away from her son's school, she turned, her face pale and drawn. 'Please.' She held up a hand. 'Just leave me alone.'

Silence fell for a moment and then the questions grew louder.

'You don't sound like a woman in love. Trouble in paradise already?'

She spun away and, despite the stultifying heat of the day, began to run. The school gates were her sanctuary—the photographers didn't cross the barrier.

How the hell had this happened? She walked towards her son's classroom, fishing her phone out of her back and loading up a browser.

With a finger that shook, she typed Dimitrios's name. The first article appeared instantly.

Billionaire Reveals Secret Love-Child and Bride-to-Be!

With a noise of disbelief, she clicked the title and scanned the first paragraph.

Renowned bachelor Dimitrios Papandreo is leaving the singles market in a move that will shock and devastate women around the world in equal measure. Rekindling a romance with his childhood sweetheart, the magnate is said to be 'looking forward' to his impending nuptials.

'When it's love, you don't want to wait.'
Love is something the tycoon has been seemingly immune to, dating often but never for long, but apparently he's finally met his match—a woman with whom he fathered a secret son six years ago!

She clicked out of the article and groaned, stuffing her phone back in her pocket. What the hell was he playing at? God, what was she going to say to Max?

Her phone began to ring and she lifted it from her pocket in the same motion with which she answered it.

'Hello?'

'Are you at Max's school?' Over the line, Dimitrios's voice took on a whole new quality. It was darker and deeper, with an even greater ability to reach inside and stir her up.

'Yes. And, thanks to you and that bloody article, I was followed here by swarming paparazzi. What the hell were you thinking?'

'The story was going to break one way or another,' he said quietly. 'I put a positive spin on it. Wouldn't you prefer our son to think we're a love match, rather than two people who couldn't control themselves?'

That pulled her up short.

'A heads-up would have been entry-level considerate.'

'Yes.' He drawled the word, so she shut her eyes, knowing that he could have said the same to her. Then, she heard him sigh. 'I didn't know when it would run. I was surprised by his efficiency. I suppose he thought I might leak the same story to a journalist from one of my own newspapers or magazines and wanted to be sure he got there first.'

That made sense, but it didn't help. 'Yeah, well, I'm at school, and Max is about to come out of his classroom, and the second we leave we're going to be mobbed by the press. I'm not ready to tell him about this, damn it, but you've made that impossible.'

'He deserves to know about me. You cannot put that off any longer. As for the paparazzi, I've sent a car.'

'What car?'

'A driver with a black SUV. He'll meet you in the teachers' car park. That should be safe from press.'

She looked over her shoulder to the path that led to the teachers' private parking area. 'I suppose so.'

'Take Max there, then go home and wait for me.'

'Wait for you to what?'

'To arrive. What does Max like to eat?'

The question was such a swift change in conversation, she almost felt as though she'd sustained whiplash. 'He's not very fussy,' she said. 'For a six-year-old. Burgers, pasta, sushi. Why?'

'I'll bring dinner. Wait until I've arrived. We'll tell him the truth together.'

He disconnected the call before she could argue—not that she was sure she wanted to. Everything had become so overwhelming and real. She felt as though the wind had completely gone from her sails.

But this wasn't a time for self-indulgence, or reflection. She needed to act now, think later. She closed the distance to Max's class room. When he emerged, she stood still and stared at him for several seconds, her heart in her throat. He was at least two inches taller than the other children, all legs and arms and intelligent eyes. His smile was quick, his face so handsome. She watched with heart-wrenching pride as a younger child stumbled and almost fell and Max, without hesitating, reached out and steadied the little girl, grinning at her before turning away. He grabbed his bag from the racks and then looked around, his eyes lighting up when he saw Annie.

He had no idea how his life was about to change.

'Hello, darling.' She tousled his hair. 'How was your day?' Such a banal question to ask when a thousand little explosions were rioting through her body and brain.

'Good. Mr Peterson said I aced our maths test'

Pride stuck in her throat. He was an excellent student. His reception teacher had suggested his academic potential might warrant skipping a year, but Annie had been of the opinion it was important for Max's social development that he spend at least a few years with children his peers in age.

'I'm not surprised by that.' She took his hand, leading him away from the class room, a lurching feeling tipping her tummy.

'Where are we going, Mummy?'

Max hadn't noticed yet, but Annie was conscious of the way other parents were looking at her. She had to get Max home.

'A friend is picking us up,' she murmured. 'This way.'

Now she understood why celebrities always wore over-sized sunglasses. What she wouldn't have done to be able to flick something down over her face! She drew Max closer, walking with an arm around his shoulders until they reached the car park.

A big, dark SUV was there, just as Dimitrios had said it would be. As they approached, two men stepped out, one from each side. The blond, wearing the very dark glasses Annie had been coveting a moment ago, moved to the rear door.

'Ma'am.' He dipped his head forward. Annie froze, the gesture of respect completely unexpected.

'Hello,' she murmured, looking into the rear to see a booster seat had been put in place.

'Who are they?' Max whispered, looking to Annie with curiosity rather than fear.

'Friends. In you go.'

She watched Max buckle himself in then crossed to the other side of the car, where the other man held the door open for her. She smiled awkwardly before taking her own seat. The car wasn't a make with which she was familiar, but she didn't need to recognise the brand to know it was clearly the last word in luxury, from the windows that were tinted as dark as night, to an expansive sun roof overhead and seats that were a sumptuous, soft black leather. There were arm rests even in the back seat and, just as Annie was marvelling at this, the man in the front passenger seat said, 'There are drinks in the centre console.'

'Drinks?' Max's expression showed how fabulous he thought that was. He flicked a switch before Annie could stop him, and the console opened to reveal small bottles of champagne, water and juice boxes. She was sorely tempted to open a champagne, anything to calm her nerves, but she knew she needed every wit about her for what was coming next.

'Can I have a juice, Mummy?'

Mummy. It pulled at her heartstrings. She opened her mouth to say no, but then realised that was silly. His world was going to change shape altogether; why deny him a rare treat when it was on offer?

'Of course.' And, to reassure him, she reached for a water bottle for herself, smiling.

She didn't live far from the school, and fortunately the paparazzi were still waiting for Max and Annie to leave the class room, which meant they were able to make a quick retreat and arrive home with no one the wiser. The car pulled up outside the front and, despite the lack of intrusive photographers, the man from the passenger seat moved quickly, coming to open Annie's door and keeping his eyes on the footpath beyond. As soon as Annie and Max were out, he shepherded them to Annie's door, standing by as it was opened. Once inside, Annie saw a dark shadow beneath the door and knew that the man was standing on the other side.

'Your friend doesn't want to come inside?' Max asked.

Annie's smile was distracted. 'No.'

'That was strange.'

'Yes.'

'Do you want to play cards?'

She blinked, the question reassuring in its normalcy.

She was about to agree when the door pushed inwards—no knock this time—and Dimitrios strode in as though he owned the place. As though he owned *every* place. She put a hand on

Max's shoulder reflexively, drawing him closer, but her eyes never left Dimitrios. He was wearing jeans today, and a simple T-shirt, white so it that showed off his tan, with a collar that sat perfectly at his neck.

'Is this another friend, Mummy?'

Annie's eyes flared wide.

'Not exactly.' She swallowed. 'Sit down, Max. There's something we want to talk to you about.'

She was conscious of everything in that moment. Of Dimitrios's size and scent as he came close to them, the smallness of her apartment, the dimness of the furnishings, their son's earnest little face, the way his uniform was tatty and faded.

'Max, this is Dimitrios,' she said quietly, taking the seat opposite Max at the dining table, watching his face for the tiniest flickers, nerves making her pulse fire. 'He was very good friends with Lewis.'

'Uncle Lewis?'

'Yes.' Annie smiled encouragingly. 'And, through Lewis, Dimitrios and I met, a long time ago. We became…friends,' she said, stumbling a little as she got closer to revealing the true nature of their relationship.

Dimitrios settled his large frame in the seat between Annie and Max, putting a hand out over Annie's. She hadn't realised until then how badly it was shaking.

'The truth is, Max, your mother and I were more than friends. We fell in love…and made you.' Every cell in her body began to reverberate. *We fell in love.* It was such a lie, but told so easily that it flared to life inside her.

'Made me?' Max frowned. 'As in, you're my dad?'

It was impossible to miss the flaring of pride in Dimitrios's eyes, or how much that statement meant to him. A wave of nausea-inducing guilt flooded her body.

'Mummy? Is that true?'

She found words almost impossible, so nodded instead.

'But you don't live with us.'

'No, I haven't lived with you,' Dimitrios responded.

'Why not?'

'I live in Singapore.' As though it were simple and that answer explained it.

And, to Annie's surprise, Max nodded. 'That's very far away, isn't it?'

'Yes. Have you ever been to Singapore?'

'I've never been on a plane. I don't even have a passport.'

Dimitrios's face angled towards Annie. 'I see.'

That wasn't so uncommon, Annie thought. It's not as though she was the only single parent in the world who'd deprived her child of an overseas holiday.

'I can organise a passport for you. How would you feel about going to Singapore?'

Annie's heart skipped a beat. She put her hand on top of Dimitrios's to quell his line of questions but he resolutely ignored her, refusing to look her way.

'I… Are we going, Mummy?'

Annie tried to smile. 'That hasn't been decided yet.'

Dimitrios leaned forward. 'The thing is, Max, I think it's time for us to be a real family—for us all to live together—and my home and work are in Singapore.'

Max tilted his head thoughtfully. 'What's your home like?'

Dimitrios's smile was pure charm. 'Would you like to see a picture?'

Max's eyes shifted to Annie's. 'Mummy? Do you want to move to Singapore?'

Annie felt Dimitrios's warning gaze, and her stomach looped with feeling. He'd lost so much—wasn't this the least she could do? Besides, her brief run-in with the paparazzi had shown her what her life was about to become. And what about Max? Didn't he deserve everything Dimitrios could give him? Didn't he deserve a father in his life?

'Singapore is lovely,' she said carefully. 'How would you feel about leaving school, though, darling?'

Max frowned, considering that, then turned to Dimitrios. 'Are there schools in Singapore?'

Dimitrios smiled gently, passing his mobile phone to the boy. 'Yes, there are excellent schools.'

'Is this...the school?' She saw Max's little mouth open in shock. Instinctively, Annie angled herself to see the phone better.

'No, Max. That's my home.'

'Your...home?' Max's eyes were huge. 'You mean I'd live there?'

'If you'd like to.'

Max returned his attention the screen. The

house was everything Annie would have imagined, if ever she'd put her mind to it—enormous, modern, huge cement-and-glass boxes piled on top of each other surrounded by tropical trees. It was clearly both impressive and expensive. Beyond it, the ocean glistened, and in the far distance, she could make out the distinctive skyline of Singapore.

'Mummy? Look.'

She nodded. She'd seen enough.

'Why haven't I met you before?'

Annie stiffened, looking at Dimitrios, her heart sinking to her toes. She searched for a way to break it to their son, to confess the decision she'd made and the consequences he'd been forced to live with. Having to confess this to Max was something she'd dreaded—and she felt the full force of what she'd been keeping from him, of the decision she'd made seven years earlier.

Dimitrios spoke before she could work out how to put her thoughts into words.

'Sometimes families become separated, Max, but, now that I'm here, I don't ever want to miss being a part of your life. I wasn't close to my dad, but I'm hoping you and I can become good friends.' His voice was deep. As an adult, she could hear the pain that underscored his words, but Max seemed to take them at face value.

Tears at Dimitrios's kindness filled Annie's eyes. How easy it would have been for him to lay the blame at her feet! To begin to drive a wedge between them, to undermine her with Max. But he didn't. If anything, he did the opposite, glossing over the details, smoothing the way for this transition without laying blame anywhere. She stood abruptly, moving into the kitchen and turning her back on them, the very act of breathing almost beyond her.

He was making everything so easy; he had all the answers. It was Annie who was left floundering, trying to decide how she could make this work, what she wanted and whether her wishes even mattered. Surely Dimitrios and Max deserved to have her put them first now, to make the whole idea of being a family work?

'You have a swimming pool?' She homed in on their conversation again, bracing her palms on the bench.

'Two swimming pools.' She heard the smile in Dimitrios's voice and her heart twisted with memories and regret.

It was the same voice he'd used the first weekend they'd met. She hadn't been much older than fifteen. He and his twin brother Zach had come to the small village on the outskirts of Sydney where she and Lewis had grown up, and Annie had felt as though her whole world had got bigger and smaller at once. She'd never known anyone like him in real life. He'd been twenty-one, but as big as a much older man, and he'd dressed like one too—expensive, classy, easy. He'd smiled at her and something inside her had changed for ever.

'Why does anyone need two swimming pools?' Max was saying with a little laugh.

'One is indoors, part of my home gym. It's for swimming laps. The other sits on the edge of my property, overlooking the bay and the city. That's more for relaxing.'

'And diving?'

Dimitrios's laugh was like warm honey running down Annie's spine. She turned quickly, needing to trap the sight of him laughing, to hold it close inside. 'Yes, for diving.' He winked at Max then his eyes moved quickly, finding Annie, and the smile on his face shifted and morphed. It stayed in place but the warmth in his eyes dropped.

Her heart turned cold.

She pulled a pint of milk from the fridge and poured Max a glass, then put a small biscuit on a plate, carrying them both back to the table.

'Do you have a suitcase?' Dimitrios was asking him.

'Mummy? Do I?'

Annie's heart squeezed with vulnerability. 'No. But we have bags,' she added, missing the look that crossed Dimitrios's eyes.

'It doesn't matter. I'll have boxes brought.'

'What for?' Max's curiosity was, as ever, insatiable.

'Packing.'

Annie startled. Packing made it all sound so real, so imminent.

'I don't have too much to pack. Mummy has hardly anything, do you, Mummy? How do we pack the sofa in a box?'

Dimitrios looked towards the small piece of furniture.

Annie cleared her throat. 'The sofa came with the apartment, dearest. It will stay here when we go.'

'Oh.' He frowned. 'But the train tracks are mine?'

Tears threatened to mist her eyes so she nodded and quickly tilted her head away. The train tracks were nothing special, but to Max they were the world.

'Why don't you go and put everything you'd like to bring on to your bed? That will make it easier to box up.'

''K.' Max finished drinking his milk then stood, smiling as he left the room.

Air had always seemed to be a stable commodity to Annie but when Dimitrios was around it developed a changeability that took her breath away. It grew thin, making it hard to focus when they were alone again. She found it difficult to meet his eyes.

'He looks so much like me.'

Annie nodded softly. 'I know.'

'I will never understand how you could choose to keep me out of his life.'

Annie's eyes swept shut. 'It wasn't an easy decision.'

'Yet you made it, every day. Even when you were struggling, and I could have made your life so much easier.'

That drew her attention. 'You think this is going to make my life easier?' A furrow developed between her brows. 'Moving to another country, *marrying* you?'

His eyes roamed her face, as though he could read things in her expression that she didn't know were there. As though her words had a secret meaning.

'Yes.'

For some reason, the confidence of his reply gave her courage. One of them, at least, seemed certain they were doing the right thing.

'What if we can't make this work, Dimitrios?'

His eyes narrowed a little. 'We will.'

It was so blithely self-assured, coming from a man who had always achieved anything he set out to, that Annie's lips curled upwards in a small smile. 'Marriage is difficult and Max is young—only six. Presuming you intend for our marriage to last until he's eighteen, that's twelve years of living together, pretending we're something we're not. I don't know about you, but the strain of that feels unbearable.'

'You're wrong on several counts, Annabelle.' He leaned forward, the noise of his movement drawing her attention, the proximity of his body making her pulse spark to life with renewed fervour. 'I intend for our marriage to be real in every way—meaning for as long as we both shall live. As for pretending we're something we're not, we don't need to do that.'

Her heart had started to beat faster. Her breath was thin. 'What exactly does a "real" marriage mean?'

'That we become a family. We live together. We share a bedroom, a bed, we raise our son as parents. It means you have my full support in every way.'

It was too much. Too much kindness and too much expectation. She'd thought he would be angry with her when he learned the truth, and that she could have handled. If he'd wanted to fight, she could have fought, but this was impossible to combat. The idea of sharing his bed... when she knew what he thought of her?

You're little more than a child, Annabelle.

He'd all but called her unsophisticated and dull, right after taking her virginity. Heat bloomed in her cheeks and she shook her head automatically.

'Sharing a home is one thing, but as for the rest—'

'You object to being a family?'

He was being deliberately obtuse.

She forced herself to be brave and say what

was on her mind. 'You think I'm going to fall back into bed with you after this many years, just because we have a son together?'

His smile was mocking, his eyes teasing. 'No, Annabelle. I think you're going to fall back into bed with me because you still want me as much as you did then. You don't need to pretend sleeping with me will be a hardship.'

Her jaw dropped and she sucked in a harsh gulp of air. 'You are so arrogant.'

His laugh was soft, his shoulders lifting in a broad shrug. 'Yes.' His eyes narrowed. 'But am I wrong?'

Deny it! Deny him! How ashamed she'd been of how easily she'd fallen into bed with him. She hadn't put up any resistance, hadn't asked him any questions. He'd come to her apartment, pulled her into his arms, and she'd simply folded herself against him, lifting her tear-stained face to be kissed better.

'You're wrong if you think I don't have more self-control than I did at eighteen,' she said quietly. 'So, far as I'm concerned, this marriage is for Max's sake alone. I don't need anything from you. I don't *want* anything from you. Behind closed doors, we'll be as we are now. No one needs to know it's all a sham.'

'Do you want it to be a sham?' he pushed quietly. 'When we know that we have the potential for this to be, in some ways, great?'

It surprised her. She didn't respond—couldn't— and waited for him to speak instead.

'Our chemistry is still there.'

Her throat felt thick; she struggled to swallow. He was just saying this to make things easier— he probably thought she'd be as easily seduced now as she'd been then. And maybe he was right. If she let him touch her, kiss her, hold her, her self-control would probably crumble into nothing, just as it had then. Which was all the more reason she had to be strong in the face of this.

'It doesn't matter,' he said after a moment, and the wave of disappointment that formed like a tsunami inside Annie showed her what a liar she was. She still wanted him every bit as much as she had then—and to him, it didn't matter.

'Sex is beside the point. But for the sake of appearances, you will be in my bedroom. Max is a child, and children talk. I don't want him going to school and telling his friends that we sleep in two separate rooms. It will expose him—and you—to the kind of gossip I'm trying to avoid.'

'But giving a journalist the scoop on Max and me is fine?'

'He already had the scoop, I simply took the opportunity to control the narrative.'

She accepted that—even the great Dimitrios Papandreo couldn't have a story in a rival newspaper pulled just because he didn't like the content.

'Then we'll have separate beds in your room. I only need a single...'

He laughed, but it wasn't a warm sound, so much as a harsh, scoffing noise.

'We will have one bed—my bed—which is big enough for you to cling to the edge of, if you're afraid I won't be able to resist reaching for you in the middle of the night.'

She felt ridiculous. Embarrassed and completely childish. And she also felt that his claim that they shared any kind of chemistry was predicated on his need to get her into his life—for the sake of Max.

He reached into his pocket, removing a small black box that he slid across the table. Annie was so caught up in her reflections that she reached for it automatically, cracking the lid with a lack of any fanfare or ceremony.

The ring deserved more.

'Wow.' She stared at it, blinked, and stared some more. 'What—is this?'

'An engagement ring.'

She lifted her eyes to his, her stomach in knots. 'It's way, way too much.'

And it was. In every way, it was ridiculously over the top. A solitaire diamond, at least the size of her thumbnail and shaped like a teardrop, sat in a four-claw platinum setting, with more diamonds running down the side of the ring—each large enough to be an earring, at least. It sparkled even in the dull light of her Sydney apartment.

'It's nothing—just what the jeweller had on hand. If you don't like it, you can choose something else.' His voice was nonchalant, as though it didn't matter to him. It was the strangest proposal Annie could imagine being a part of. This whole situation was bizarre.

'I like it,' she responded with a small shift of her head. 'It's just—how much did this cost?' Then, another shake of her head. 'Never mind, don't tell me. I don't want to know.' She pursed her lips, searching for words. 'Can you see how difficult life has been for me? I've scrimped and saved to be able to afford the things Max wants, and even then always had to buy him second-hand or cheap copies, and you swoop in here with something like this… It's going to take me a while to get my head around it all.'

'You should have contacted me.'

I tried. She kept the fact buried inside herself. It would feel like revealing too much of her feelings, as they'd been then. She didn't want to discuss the past in that kind of detail.

'The pre-nuptial agreement.' He pulled it out of his other pocket and slid it across the table top. 'You should consult a lawyer, of course, but they won't find anything wrong with it. The terms are very favourable to you.'

'I can't afford a lawyer,' she said with a groan of frustration. 'I barely know how I'm going to pay for our electricity bill so please just…' She shook her head, not sure what she'd wanted to say. 'Explain it to me.'

A muscle jerked at the base of his jaw but he nodded.

'It's simple. Max's trust fund is detailed in the first two paragraphs. The next deals with what happens if I die—how my wealth is distributed into trusts for him and any other children we might have.' Heat ran like lava through her veins. 'Finally, there's the matter of your allowance and settlement in the event of a divorce.'

Her eyes focussed on that paragraph. Divorce. Her head was spinning. Just like that, it was a foregone conclusion that she would marry him, and he was even planning how they'd deal with a possible divorce.

She forced herself to read the terms carefully, then blinked up at him. 'This looks like I get a ridiculously generous allowance for as long as we're married, and not a lot if I decide to leave you.'

His eyes were business-like. She remembered an article she'd read a few years back, calling him 'a ruthless tycoon'. It was the perfect description for him in that moment.

'That's the point.'

'What is?'

'Your life, as my wife, will be beyond anything you can imagine. You will have whatever you want, whenever you want it.'

It was what he *didn't* say that sent a shiver down her spine. 'And if I leave you I get nothing, and have to live like this again?'

He looked around her apartment, his eyes narrowed. 'You will never live like this again.' His anger was unmistakable. 'But you will definitely find it undesirable to walk away from me.'

'You plan to keep me as what—some kind of economic prisoner?'

'I won't reward you for leaving our marriage; that's not the same thing.'

She swallowed a curse.

He reached across, putting his hand on hers, surprising her with the touch. 'I want our marriage to last a lifetime, for Max's sake.'

What did any of this matter? If they divorced, she wouldn't want any of his money. Pride wouldn't allow her to take it. She'd sooner live in a tiny flat like this again than exist on handouts from Dimitrios.

Tilting her chin in a gesture of defiance, she nodded. 'Fine. I'll sign it.'

His eyes flared with victory. Keeping one hand on hers, he used his other to lift the ring from the box and slowly push it on to her wedding finger.

'It's the right decision.'

Dimitrios stared out at Sydney CBD from his penthouse apartment right at the top of Papandreo Towers, a frown on his handsome face. It was the right decision. There was nothing else he could do. *Support her financially?* an inner voice challenged him. *Sure. But then what?* See their son only occasionally? Be an absent father or, worse, force Annabelle to be an absent mother? Neither option was palatable, and he didn't have to dig very deep into his psyche to understand why.

It was history repeating itself. When he'd walked into her tiny, insalubrious flat, he'd been reminded of the first ten years of his own life, spent living in abject poverty with a mother who'd tried her best but still hadn't been able to keep them afloat. His childhood had been punctuated by contrasts. When his father had occasionally appeared in Dimitrios and Zach's life, he'd whisk them away for a week of luxury and grandeur—everything they wanted was theirs, only to have it all disappear when they'd returned to their mother's. The visits were always fleeting, unpredictable and, as Dimitrios had got older, infuriating. How could his father have so much and leave their mother with so little?

It wasn't as though Dimitrios had ever consciously promised himself he would avoid that situation but, finding himself in his father's shoes, he was determined to act in a way that was in complete contrast to his father's behaviour. He wouldn't see Annabelle suffer. He wouldn't see her worry about money for another moment.

And their son would never feel that he had to love either his father or his mother, but never both. They would be a united front for the sake of Max.

Annabelle might want to resist that, but Dimitrios understood something she wanted far more. It was in her eyes when she looked at him, in the way her body swayed towards him when they were close, in the way her breath grew rushed and her cheeks pink.

She wanted him just as much as she had the night they'd conceived Max—and Dimitrios intended to remind her of that, night by seductive night, until their marriage of necessity developed into something that would bind them in a more meaningful way. Bit by bit, he'd remind her of what they'd shared, and make it impossible for her to contemplate leaving him. All for the sake of their son.

CHAPTER FOUR

Nineteen years earlier

'WHAT HAPPENED THEN, *Lou-Lou?*'

'I've asked you not to call me that.' Her older brother softened the admonition with a gentle shoulder-nudge, then grinned.

'Lewis,' Annie corrected, practising the eye-roll she'd been working on.

Lewis laughed. 'Better.' He lay back on the bed, flexing his hands behind his head. 'Well, let's see. The Princess escaped the tower and rode the dragon to safety.'

'Uh-huh. And the dragon promised not to burn her?'

'Because she's a princess.'

'Uh-huh.'

'So that must just leave the bit with the Prince.'

Six-year-old Annie lifted up on her elbow, pouting as she studied Lewis's face. At twelve, he could have been busy playing football, or reading the books he loved, but instead he always told Annie a personalised bed-time story. It was their ritual.

'Yes?' Annie asked, waiting.

'Well, the dragon brought the Princess down to a field—'

'What kind of field?'

'Does it matter?'

'Flowers? Wheat? Corn?'

Lewis grinned. 'Flowers.'

'Okay. Purple flowers?'

'Sure, Annie. Purple flowers.'

She smiled at that, flopping back on to the bed and looking up at the ceiling. Her eyes felt heavy.

'He brought her into the field and there, waiting for her, was the Prince Charming she'd heard so much about. Now that she was free from the Evil Queen, nothing could stop them from getting married and ruling the kingdom side by side. They lived happily ever after.'

Annie smiled. They always lived happily ever after.

'Lewis, are princesses and princes real?'

'Sure they are.'

'But I'm not really a princess?'

'You are to me.'

She smiled, her eyes sweeping closed.

'And will I grow up to marry a prince?'

'Well, he might not be a real prince, but he'll treat you like a princess or he'll have me to deal with.'

'I saw it.' Dimitrios's lips were set in a grim line. His brother looked back at him from the screen of the tablet.

'Has Annie?'

Dimitrios cast an eye towards the newspaper folded on his dining table. The headline was like all the others—proclaiming the secret relationship and love child. But the article had been a barely concealed attack on Annabelle, calling her everything from 'frumpy' to 'ordinary' to 'struggling single mother'. Of course, they'd chosen a particularly unflattering photograph of her, taken the day before. Even then, Dimitrios found his eyes lingering on the picture, noticing all the things the journalist had obviously missed. The elegance of her neck as she spun to address the paparazzi, the sheen of her hair—so shimmering it was like gold—the poise and determination in the strength of her spine, the fullness of her lips, the depth of her eyes.

He pushed the paper aside and gave Zach the full force of his attention.

'Well?'

'I don't know.' Dimitrios ground his teeth together. 'But, either way, she'll have to get used to that kind of crass reporting. It's part and parcel of being a Papandreo.'

'And she's okay with that?'

Dimitrios paused, his brother's hesitation pulling at something inside him. 'What's that supposed to mean?'

'Come on, Dim. You might have the rest of the world fooled with the "sweethearts reunited" bit but not me. You guys were never an item.' Zach laughed softly. 'Well, with the obvious exception of one night.'

Dimitrios instinctively recoiled from discussing Annabelle, even with his brother.

'That's irrelevant. We have a son together.'

'And I can't wait to meet him, but you can't let Annie be torn apart in the media like this. She doesn't deserve that.'

Dimitrios fought an instinct to point out that Annabelle had kept his son from him for six years. 'No,' he agreed. 'I have very little control of how rival media outlets decide to spin this story, though.'

'You have control of a lot more than you realise. You just need to make it much harder for her to be criticised; take the wind out of their sails. Change the story, Dimitrios, for Annie's sake.'

Annie woke with a start, a terrible feeling in her gut that perhaps she'd overslept. It was just like in high school, when there had been an exam or assessment and she used to wake in the mornings convinced she'd missed it. But there was no exam. Just the rest of her life waiting for her. And the anxiety she felt was like a whole ball of wool knotted in her belly. She pushed out of bed and was crossing the apartment to the small bathroom when there was a knock at the door. A glance at her watch showed the time to be almost seven.

She was about to open it when she remembered the intrusion of the press the day before, and Dimitrios's parting warning: 'They will be waiting for you tomorrow. I'll send a driver, but be aware—there will be questions.'

At the door, she paused. 'Who is it?'

'Henderson, ma'am. I drove you home yesterday.'

Surely it was way too early for the driver to take them to school. She flicked a glance at the clock and groaned. It *wasn't* too early. She *had* overslept. With a small yelp, she pulled the door inwards, keeping her pyjama-clad body concealed behind it. 'We just need a few minutes, okay?'

'Of course.' He nodded.

'Would you like to come in? Help yourself to some water or tea?' She thought longingly of the last two teabags sitting in the bottom of the canister.

'There's coffee in the car, ma'am.'

Coffee! Her heart leaped at the promise of caffeine. She smiled. 'Thank you. We won't be long.'

She ran across the apartment, throwing open the door to Max's room. And it hit her the second she saw the plastic grocery bags filled with his dearest possessions.

This was happening.

They were leaving.

Pushing away all the consequences that came

with that, she moved to the bed, pressing a kiss to his forehead. 'Time to wake up, Max. We're late.'

'Are we?' he mumbled, so beautifully sleepy, her heart clutched.

'Yep. Can you get dressed straight away?'

'Yes, Mummy.'

She readied herself quickly, throwing on a pair of jeans and a loose-fitting black shirt, noting that it was a little looser than usual. *You look like you haven't eaten in a week.* She frowned as she took a few moments to look at her reflection in the mirror. She had lost weight lately. Too much weight, and not as a result of trying. Her teeth bit down on her lower lip. She tucked the shirt in. That was even worse. She pulled it out, leaving it loose, and added a big bright necklace she'd bought at a charity shop around the corner.

Slightly better.

Hair pulled into a topknot, a piece of toast thrust into Max's hand to eat in the car, and they were ready.

Except—how could they ever *really* be ready? The second they stepped a few feet from the apartment, flashes went off and the questions began again—this time, directed at Max.

'Max, how do you feel about your dad?'

'Are you looking forward to the wedding?'

'Have you spent much time with him?'

'Is it true you have twin brothers as well?'

At that, Annie sent a scowl to the journalist and leaned down closer to Max. 'Don't answer them, dearest. Just go straight to the car.'

Henderson put a strong arm around the pair and shepherded them to the waiting SUV, standing to block the photographers' view as they stepped in. With the door closed, they were protected by the darkly tinted windows.

'That was weird,' Max commented, wrinkling his nose.

Annie burst out laughing. 'Yes, that's one word for it.' She kept laughing because it felt good, and because she was glad for her son's resilience and calmness. She reached across, squeezing his hand.

'Look, Mummy,' Max said as the car pulled out from the kerb. 'There are drinks again.'

'Coffee,' she remembered. 'And that looks like a hot chocolate for you.'

'Really? Are you sure?' His eyes darted nervously towards the front of the car.

Her heart tightened in her chest. 'Yes, I'm sure.'

His eyes lit up as he reached for the cup, blowing across the top before taking a sip. His smile was the only response Annie needed. He ate his toast and drank his hot chocolate, clearly feeling very special as they drove to school. At the gates, Annie walked him in as normal, though nothing *felt* normal. Parents—even parents she considered her friends—were regarding her strangely, and Max's teacher looked as though she wanted to ask a thousand and one questions.

Annie's manner was not expansive. She crouched down, lifting a hand to Max's face, brushing away his thick, dark fringe.

'It's probably best if you don't talk too much about all the changes, Max. There'll be plenty of time to explain to your friends, but why don't we let the dust settle first?'

He nodded. 'Okay.' His nose wrinkled. 'I don't think I'd know what to say, anyway.'

Something inside her ached. She felt his vulnerability in myriad ways. 'No,' she said quietly, roughing his hair. 'You know you can ask me any question at any time, don't you?'

He nodded thoughtfully. 'I know.'

Annie kept her head ducked as she left school, not wanting to engage in conversation with anyone. Henderson was waiting beside the car, arms crossed.

She strapped herself in, pushing her head against the leather head-rest, her eyes closed.

It took a few moments before Annie realised the car was travelling in the wrong direction. She frowned, leaning forward. 'Where are we going?'

'Mr Papandreo asked me to bring you to him.'

To bring you to him. As though she were a possession. 'It would have been nice for him to ask *me* first,' she said under her breath, though a quick glance in the rear-view mirror showed the remnants of a smile on Henderson's face—confirming he'd heard her comment.

She sighed softly. How was she going to avoid snapping at Dimitrios when he was so…so…overbearing? Most people would naturally seek approval before organising someone's schedule, but not Dimitrios. He told a member of his staff to 'bring her to him', without considering that she might have other plans or might simply not want to 'go to him'.

Her eyes fell to her tightly clasped hands sitting in her lap, and the enormous diamond on her finger sparkled brightly.

It was rush hour, and traffic was thick, but the SUV dug through the cars, drawing Annie deeper into a gridded city cast into shade by the glass-and-steel monoliths that towered overhead. She didn't come into the CBD often, so found it hard to get her bearings. Eventually, the car stopped—she thought she caught a glimpse of a sign that read 'Castlereagh Street'. The door was opened and Annie stepped out, breathing in that unique city smell of bitumen, leather, engine exhaust and corporate toil.

'This way, ma'am.'

She smiled hesitantly. 'Henderson, if you're going to be driving me regularly, would you consider calling me Annie?'

He didn't respond.

'After all, you look about my age. It feels ridiculously stuffy for you to be calling me "ma'am".'

'Is it making you uncomfortable?'

'Honestly, yes. It really is.'

He laughed softly. 'Fine. Miss Hargreaves.'

'No.' She shook her head. 'Just Annie. I'm begging you.'

He lifted his sunglasses so she could see his

eyes—one was blue and the other brown. 'Fine, Annie. If you insist.'

'I do.' It was a small victory, but it felt important that Annie should hold on to the essence of who she was for as long as possible. 'Thank you. Now, where's Dimitrios?'

With a nod, Henderson gestured to a pair of shiny black glass doors. Annie stopped walking, her breath hitching in her throat as she read the word boldly emblazoned in the signage above. The name was world-famous, synonymous with luxury and prestige. It was the kind of shop she'd never even walked past, far less thought of entering.

'Why?' she asked Henderson, a tone of pleading in her voice.

Henderson smiled, but didn't respond.

Annie stifled a groan but started walking once more, one foot in front of the other, until they reached the doors. Henderson lifted his hand to a buzzer, pressed it and then they waited.

It took only a couple of seconds before the doors whooshed inwards, revealing a shining floor made of large marble tiles, high ceilings, ornate chandeliers dangling from the ceiling and an army of at least ten staff standing in a group.

And beside them, Dimitrios, impeccably dressed in one of his custom-made suits with shining shoes, dark hair waved back from his brow, eyes on Annie with a singular focus that made a hint of perspiration form in the valley of her breasts. She was grateful then for Henderson at her side.

'Annabelle.' Dimitrios strode towards her, drawing her into his arms. His eyes glittered with hers, giving Annie only a moment of warning before he dropped his head and crushed his lips to hers, kissing her with an excellent approximation of fierce possession.

She knew it was just for the benefit of their audience, but that didn't change anything. She felt the flicker of desire in the pit of her stomach and, before she could stop it, full-blown need was coursing through her veins. Her arms lifted of their own accord, one hand pressing to his chest, the other curling around the nape of his neck, her fingers teasing the dark hair there, holding him where he was. His tongue expertly duelled with hers, reminding her of his mastery over her, the ease with which he'd driven her senseless with longing all those years ago.

That should have been enough of a reminder. It should have made her put an end to the kiss. But her body was in complete control and it wanted him with a ferocity that was too hard to bear.

His arm curved around her back, as though he knew she needed his support, and he held her there as he lifted his head, his eyes boring into hers, his expression impossible to interpret. But his cheeks were darker than normal, slashed along the ridges of his bones, and she knew he had been as stirred by their kiss as she had been.

'What was that?' she asked, wishing she felt angrier, more outraged, when all she could muster was disbelief that it had ended so quickly.

'Remember, *agape*,' he said quietly, then lowered his head so only she could hear the rest of his sentence. 'All the world believes this is a love match. Try to play along.'

It was the ice water she needed, the stark dose of reality to bring sense back to her addled mind.

'Of course, darling.' She mimicked his tone, forcing an over-bright smile to her face.

'Thank you for meeting me here,' he murmured, taking hold of her hand and weaving their fingers together.

'Did I have a choice?' she queried, without letting her smile drop, her voice just a whisper.

His eyes held a warning. 'Not really.'

He began to walk towards the staff, who had been discreetly looking away from the couple. A man stepped forward. 'Madam, it is a pleasure to meet you. My name is Gustav and I am the manager of the Sydney store. Mr Papandreo has asked me to help you this morning with anything you might require.'

Annie wrinkled her nose, looking around the high-end boutique with a burgeoning and unwelcome sense of inadequacy. 'Honestly, I don't know how you can help me,' she said quietly. 'I don't really shop in places like this.'

'Then that has been our loss,' the manager inserted charmingly. 'Now, let's get to work.'

All the staff scattered except the manager, who asked Annie, 'Now, champagne and an almond croissant?'

It was on the tip of her tongue to point out that it was just after nine o'clock in the morning, when she thought about how welcome a glass of bubbly would be, given the over-wrought state of her nerves. 'Just a little,' she conceded, nodding a little.

'Excellent. And for you, sir?'

'Coffee.'

'Very good.'

When the manager disappeared, they were completely alone, Henderson waited by the doors with his arms crossed, the last word in forbidding.

'Where are all the other customers?'

'The store isn't open yet.'

'I beg to differ.' She gestured to the staff working to pull dresses, shirts and shoes from racks, transporting them all through a pair of silver velvet curtains.

'They've opened early.'

'For you?'

'For *you*,' he corrected.

'Dimitrios.' She sighed, biting down on her lip. 'Why are you doing this?'

His hand reached for the collar of her T-shirt, pulling on it gently. 'Because your clothes are somewhat the worse for wear, and because I can. Because you're going to be my wife and you will need to dress like it. Because I get the feeling you've sacrificed every comfort for yourself over the years just so that my son can have what he needs most.'

She looked up at him, finding his answers strangely breath-taking. She was both embarrassed that he thought so little of her appearance and touched that he understood how miniscule her budget was for her own clothes.

'It's been hard,' she said quietly. 'But this is too much. I don't need...' She reached for the nearest piece of clothing, a pale-pink blouse made of silk with pearl buttons. The price almost made her fall sideways. 'Dimitrios, this is ridiculous. Who pays this for a shirt, for goodness' sake?'

He unfurled her fingers from the fabric, then drew her to his side. It was all an act, for the benefit of the staff, but his nearness set warm arrows darting through her body.

'Don't think about the price. Just buy whatever you want.'

She shook her head. 'But I don't want anything. I know my clothes aren't exactly glamorous but they're perfect for *me*. For my lifestyle. I work from home. I take Max to school. And, whether we're here or in Singapore, I can't see that changing.'

'Last week, the American President came for dinner,' he said, his voice devoid of emotion. 'I entertain guests like him regularly. Tell me, Annabelle, what do you have that you would wear to a meal with the President?'

She forced herself not to show how awed she

was by that. He was trying to scare her into obedience but that made it all the more important that Annie remember who she was. 'I'd wear whatever I had that was clean, and a smile on my face, and I'd ask him about his trip to Singapore and his family, and that would be the end of it.'

Admiration showed on his face. 'I'm not asking you to swan around the house in ball gowns.' His tone was now one of gentle coercion. 'Just try a few things on…see what you like. If you decide you don't want anything at the end of the morning, then that's fine.'

Gustav returned with a glass so full of champagne it had formed a meniscus. He carried it on a small silver tray. 'Madam.'

'Please, call me Annie,' she insisted as she took the champagne.

'Yes, Annie. And coffee, sir.'

Dimitrios nodded curtly as he took the cup, making the fine porcelain look unspeakably tiny in his tanned, masculine hand.

His eyes held both a question and a warning. Annie could stand there and argue some more or she could just surrender to this process, try a few dresses on and then tell him thanks, but no thanks. After all, she wasn't his charity project.

She could take her admittedly meagre savings to a department store and buy some new clothes, now that she knew her immediate worries—such as having food on the table—were taken care of.

It was clear that the sales assistants were skilled professionals. The first thing Annie tried on was a linen dress in a colour just like lemon curd. She was only doing it to be obliging, but the second she slipped the dress over her body she felt something click in place. She stared at her reflection for at least ten seconds before reaching for the glass of champagne and taking a large gulp, unable to shift her eyes away.

She looked…like she used to look. She'd never worn anything this beautiful, of course, but the dress brought out the youthfulness of her complexion, reminding her that she was, in fact, only twenty-five.

She stepped out of it quickly, feeling as though the beautiful dress had betrayed her intention not to want any of these designer clothes. White trousers were next, and they were just as flattering. A black-and-white spotty dress followed, then a silk camisole paired with a denim skirt, showing Annie's slim, tanned legs. An hour passed in a flurry of silk, linen, cotton and chiffon and, unbeknownst to her, a diligent Gustav was piling each outfit she'd tried on beside the cash register. When Annie finally emerged from the sumptuous fitting room—back in her regular clothes—her champagne was empty and her resolve was beginning to soften just a little.

'Well?' Dimitrios approached her with a knowing look on his face. 'Let me guess. You loved them all?'

She *had* loved them all, but she knew to buy all of them would be unspeakably extravagant. 'I did. But I particularly loved the yellow dress,' she qualified, moving towards it and running her fingers lovingly over the fabric. 'It was… beautiful.'

For a moment, she thought she saw surprise in the depth of his eyes.

'Then you'll have it.' He removed it from the rack. 'Why don't you wear it today? It's appropriate for your next appointment.'

'Next appointment?' Despite his generosity, something bristled inside her at his high-handed management of her schedule.

'A day spa.'

If she'd had champagne in her mouth she would have spurted it everywhere. Her scepticism must have showed because he leaned closer, murmuring, 'Try it. Just this once. For me.'

She was about to scoff at that but the fact they were being watched meant she had to alter her natural response. 'For you, darling? Anything.'

He dropped his head closer, his eyes warring with hers in a way that set her pulse racing. 'Careful, Annabelle. I just might hold you to that later.'

CHAPTER FIVE

SHE'D RESENTED HIS control-freak ways but, deep down, Annie had to admit that, up until a moment ago, she had also felt a mixture of gratitude and appreciation for Dimitrios. She'd thought the day spa was a gesture of great kindness and compassion, and she'd even let herself enjoy the experience—a full-body massage, a manicure, a pedicure and finally an appointment with the country's top hairstylist. Her natural blonde mane had been given a few foils then toned to a glossy gold and trimmed a little so that the edges were soft, and the layers gave her hair more bounce.

She emerged from the spa feeling a million times better than she had before.

But when Henderson drove her back towards Sydney, he bypassed the turn-off to her suburb completely, causing Annie to lean forward and question him.

'Boss's directions.'

Boss's directions? She sat back in her seat, crossing her arms over her chest, and waited to see what Dimitrios had in store for her next.

'But Max—'

'He's being picked up by one of my colleagues.'

Annie's chest squeezed. In all of Max's life, she'd never once missed a school pick-up. The thought of doing so now filled her with a sense of disbelief.

'But…why?' She shook her head. 'Don't tell me. Dimitrios.'

'Sorry, miss—Annie.'

He drove the car into an underground parking garage, dark despite the fact it was a bright afternoon. She caught a brief glimpse of a sign that read 'Papandreo Towers'.

Henderson accompanied her in the lift but when the doors pinged open on the very top floor he remained behind.

'You're not coming in?'

'No, Annie. Good evening.'

It was strange that she'd come to think of his company as reassuring, but somehow knowing he was just like her—a normal person, rather than someone born into this kind of wealth—made him a touchstone to the real world.

Dimitrios Papandreo was definitely not that.

She stepped into the penthouse and felt like a fish a thousand feet out of water.

'Oh, wow.' She stopped still, standing where she was and angling her face to take in the details of the incredible space. Floor-to-ceiling windows framed one of the most dramatic views of Sydney she'd ever seen, and the ceilings had to be at least treble normal height. There was a polished white marble staircase in the centre of the room that swept elegantly towards a mezzanine level; she presumed bedrooms were up there. A baby grand piano stood in one corner. The artwork on the walls was priceless, and the kitchen looked as though it belonged in the pages of a glossy magazine.

Then, there was Dimitrios, so perfectly at home in the luxurious setting, despite the fact he'd discarded his suit jacket and tie and had unbuttoned the top of his shirt to reveal the tanned column of his neck.

She'd been annoyed at him a moment ago, hadn't she? Yes! *Hold on to that.*

'Why did you bring me here?'

It wasn't exactly what she'd meant to ask but it was a start.

'It's going to be our home until the wedding.'

More high-handedness! She ground her teeth together. 'I already have a home.'

He made a noise of disapproval. 'I made arrangements. Your landlord was happy to end your lease early, given our circumstances.'

'But—' She stared at him, gobsmacked. 'You've spoken to my landlord?'

'Of course.'

'No, *not* of course!' She sighed in exasperation. 'He's *my* landlord. It's *my* lease. *My* home.'

Dimitrios took a step towards her. '*My* son. *My* fiancée. *My* responsibility.'

His responsibility. In a way, it was just what she needed to hear, because all day she'd been wondering why he was going to so much effort, spoiling her with a day spa and a shopping spree. But of course—he felt guilty. He saw her as his responsibility and in some kind of moralistic way felt as though he'd let her down these past six years by not supporting her more. When the opposite was true—she'd let him down by not allowing him a chance to know his son.

The fight left her as guilt rose within her chest.

'Okay.' She nodded once. 'Fine. We'll live here.'

His frown was a whip across his face. 'I expected more of an argument.'

Her smile was just a whisper. 'So did I.'

Her response had clearly made him uncertain, but then, this was Dimitrios Papandreo, and uncertainty wasn't something he did very well. A moment later, he shrugged, evidently taking her decision as a win. 'Great. Your things have been moved into my room upstairs. Max has a room down the corridor from us. In Singapore, there's more space than this; you can have your own sitting room and courtyard for privacy. Max will have a sitting room too.'

'More space than this?' And suddenly, Annie was laughing, because it was all so preposterous. 'This place is... Don't you see, Dimitrios? It's like a palace.'

'That's relative,' he said with a small nod. 'To you, it would seem that way.'

She felt instantly gauche. She sobered, moving into the kitchen, opening drawers and doors on autopilot, though not looking for anything in particular. When she saw the kettle in a cupboard, she lifted it out and filled it with water, simply because it felt good to have something to do with her hands.

'Who's collecting Max from school?'

'My driver, and a nanny.'

'A nanny?' Her head jerked towards his. 'What do you mean, a nanny?'

'Don't look at me like that. I'm not seeking to replace you in his life. I thought an extra pair of hands would be useful during the transition. There'll be a lot of changes. Her name's Francesca and she'll help both of you…adapt.'

The sound of the kettle boiling filled the room. Annie stared at the wisps of steam that lifted from it, her mind reeling. This was all happening so fast; she felt as if she'd barely drawn breath since Dimitrios had reappeared in her life. Had it really only been a matter of days?

'I thought we could use this time to discuss the wedding.'

The knots pulled tighter. 'If you'd like.'

She heard his exhalation of breath but didn't turn to face him. 'Would you like tea?'

'I'll make coffee.'

She nodded, busying herself preparing tea, working beside him in the kitchen in what was a bizarrely ordinary task of domesticity. It was as if they were long-term partners, undertaking such routine, normal duties as though they did them often.

When her tea was made, she propped her bottom against the edge of the kitchen bench, her huge blue eyes framed by thick black lashes, her cheeks pink, her newly styled hair sitting like a pale, fluffy cloud around her face. He mirrored her action, standing opposite her, coffee cup in hand, eyes on her face.

The silence was far from comfortable. She felt every second that passed pull harder on her nerves, until they felt stretched near to breaking point.

'So?' she prompted eventually, when she couldn't take it any more.

'So.' He dragged his free hand through his hair. 'I've arranged the wedding for Friday. Zach's coming. I know you're not close, but I presume you'd still like your parents to be there?'

Annie's stomach dropped. 'My parents?'

Dimitrios studied her. 'Yes.'

'No.' It was a knee-jerk response. 'They don't need to be involved in this.' Her tongue darted out to lick her lower lip. 'They're over in Perth and we're here...'

'You're sure?'

She nodded jerkily. 'Let's just keep it small. A quick, private ceremony.'

His eyes didn't leave her face. He watched her for several long seconds.

'Like ripping off a sticking plaster?' he prompted, with a hint of mocking amusement.

'Yes.' She was relieved, though.

'I know this isn't what either of us would have chosen, but it's the right thing to do.'

Butterflies rampaged through her belly. She nodded, almost convinced he was right.

'So why do you look as though you're about to have a root canal?'

Her eyes flew wide. 'Do I?'

'Or worse,' he said quietly, straightening and taking a step towards her. 'Is the idea of marrying me really so appalling to you?'

Her eyes scanned his face, her heart slamming into her rib cage with the force of a freight train. Annie contemplated it, trying to find words to express how she felt.

'It's just very sudden,' she said eventually.

'For us both,' he pointed out, closing the distance between them, coming to stand toe-to-toe, bracing his arms on either side of her, his body caging hers. Her heart moved faster and harder for a different reason now, reminding her of how it had felt to be in his arms at the boutique that morning, pressed hard against him, his mouth on hers. Her gaze dropped to his lips and her own parted in memory and need.

'There's so much I don't know about you.'

'And what you do know, you don't like?' he suggested.

Her pulse fired. He was right. She had been angry with him for a long time—her heart broken, her feelings hurt. But that all seemed so long ago. Seven years was a long time in anyone's life but for Annie, with all she'd had to keep her busy, the trials she'd faced every day, it had been like a lifetime.

'The truth is, I barely know you.'

Was that really the truth? Standing like this, she felt as though he was familiar to her in an elemental way. Memories of the night they'd spent together were hovering on the brink of her mind, as though they'd happened only a night or so ago, not seven years.

'You'll get to know me.'

'And to like you?'

'That would make our marriage easier,' he said with a tight smile.

Perhaps. Perhaps not. The difficulty, though, wasn't in liking him—it was in liking him too much. She needed to keep some perspective and remember that this was all for Max's sake. Whatever girlhood infatuation she'd felt for Dimitrios, that was in the distant past. The last thing she should do was let her physical response to him make her forget the truth of their situation.

'What time will Max be home?'

His eyes narrowed. 'Soon.'

She was glad. Max was a talisman of reality. 'We should get this over with, then.'

He lifted a brow and she realised the way he could misconstrue her words. Heat flamed in her cheeks. 'Firming up on the details, I mean.'

'Of course.' His response was tongue-in-cheek. She felt as if he was mocking her.

'So the wedding will be on Friday?'

He nodded, apparently back to being business-like, but he didn't move his body. Traitorous feelings made her glad.

'In the morning. I thought we'd fly to Singapore straight after lunch.'

Her breath snagged in her throat. 'So soon?'

'Why delay? Unless you'd prefer we took a honeymoon first?'

A honeymoon conjured exactly the kind of imagery she wished to avoid. She shook her head quickly. His smile showed he understood.

'Are you afraid of me, Annabelle?' His fingers caught her chin, gently lifting her face towards his so he could read her eyes.

Her lips parted, words trapped inside her.

'Or are you afraid of wanting me, even after all this time?'

Her eyes widened at his perceptive powers. Or perhaps she was just that painstakingly obvious.

Her throat moved as she swallowed. 'I'm not afraid of anything.'

His laugh was silent, just a movement of his lips and a release of his warm breath. It fanned her temple. Her insides shifted; her lungs squeezed.

'When I kissed you today it felt as though no time had passed.'

That was exactly how it had been for her, too!

'It was just playing a part,' she reminded him, but the words came out high-pitched.

'No, it was more than that. It's the saving grace of what we're doing. You don't know me, and I don't know you, but our bodies are in sync, and that's something. It's enough, for now, to base our marriage on. Don't bother denying that you feel it too.'

Was that what she'd been doing?

She shook her head a little, losing herself in the magnetic depths of his eyes. 'I don't want to feel anything for you,' she said quietly.

'Why not?' His thumb padded her lower lip, sending little shivers of desire through her.

'Because.'

One side of his lip lifted in a curl that could have been amusement or cynicism. 'That's not really an answer.'

'I know.'

'You're still angry with me for what I said to you seven years ago?'

Old wounds festered deep inside her. 'I'm not still angry,' she said quietly. 'But I'm smarter now than I was then. I learned my lesson.'

'What lesson is that?'

'Play with fire and you're bound to get burned.'

'Am I fire?'

'You were for me.'

'And I burned you?'

His head was moving closer with every word he spoke, so his lips were only a hair's-breadth from hers. 'You changed me,' she said quietly.

'How?'

She could hardly think straight. 'You taught me not to take things at face value.'

'Why?'

'Because I thought you wanted more from me than just—sex.'

His frown was a slash on his features. 'I wanted to share our grief.'

'Yes,' she agreed. 'But you didn't really want *me*. Any woman would have done for that.'

His response was to move his whole body closer, so she felt his hardness against her, his arousal against her belly. Her stomach looped.

'And you already had a girlfriend,' she added quickly.

'No,' he said.

'But you said—'

'I said what I needed to make sure you got the message. At the time, I thought I was looking out for you, pushing you away for your own good. I didn't want you thinking there was any future for us so I told you what I thought would scare you off.'

Surprise shifted her features. 'You lied to me?'

His expression was impossible to interpret.

'And that lie cost me. If I hadn't said that, would you have tried to tell me about Max?'

The world was falling away from them; Annie felt as though she were standing on an island with only Dimitrios, their history forming a swirling, raging ocean on all sides. She lifted a hand, curling her fingers in the fabric of his shirt, feeling the warmth of his body through her fingertips.

She'd intended to push him away but, just for the moment, the proximity and warmth of him flowed through her, his strength pushing into her body.

'I did try to tell you.'

The words were softly spoken, so Dimitrios had to focus to make sure he'd understood her. *I did try to tell you.* Was she lying, to justify the fact he had a six-year-old child he'd only just learned about?

'After I found out I was pregnant, I came to tell you, but…'

He was finding it hard to breathe. 'But?'

'I saw you with all your friends, and some woman—who I presumed to be your girlfriend— and I just couldn't do it.' Her voice was hollow, as though she were speaking to him from a long way away. 'You were so sophisticated, it was like you belonged to a whole other universe than the one I lived in. I was only eighteen, Dimitrios. I was scared and embarrassed, and I had no idea what you'd say, but I knew you already had a pretty low opinion of me.'

His gut tightened. 'Where was this?'

'At some bar. I'd seen in the papers that you were going to the opening. You'd been involved in funding it or something.'

He remembered. It was a place on Circular Quay. 'I wish I had told you then.' He could hear the sincerity in her voice and it pulled at something inside him. Whatever anger he was still nursing towards her shifted. 'If it happened now, I would.'

'You were young,' he pointed out.

'Like the child you accused me of being?'

That had been wrong. At the time, she'd felt like a child, but so much of that had been tied up in his guilt. Guilt at sleeping with Lewis's younger sister. If Lewis had been alive, it would never have happened. Lewis would have killed Dimitrios. He'd adored Annabelle—or 'Annie'—and had spoken of her often. Dimitrios had been aware that she had a bit of a crush on him, but he'd never planned to do anything to encourage it. So why the hell had he found his way to her door that night? Why had he pulled her into his arms and kissed her until all thoughts of Lewis, death and sadness were obliterated from his mind?

She didn't wait for an answer. 'I did want to tell you. But then I saw you with that woman and I was—hurt. Jealous.' She shook her head, not quite meeting his eyes. 'I know I had no right to feel that way...'

He lifted his hands, cupping her face. 'Whatever else we were, I was your first lover. It's natural that you felt something when you saw me with another woman so soon after that night.'

Her lower lip trembled, and he groaned, because he didn't want her to cry. He needed her not to.

'I thought I'd be ruining your life because I'd fallen pregnant. Then I thought you might insist on taking the baby away from me. I was hormonal and alone and it was hard to know what to do. But, the more time that passed, the more I felt I'd done the right thing. Until he was born... and he just looked so much like you, Dimitrios.

His eyes were exactly like yours.' Her voice was hoarse, thickened by emotion.

'I thought about telling you then. I even picked up my phone to call you, but the things you'd said to me that night kept going around and around my head.'

He stiffened, anger at the past making his body grow tense.

'I don't mean that I wanted to keep it a secret to punish you. But you were so cold that night. I felt like you…hated me. What if you hated our baby, too? What if you hated me even more for having him? I honestly felt like my only option was to keep him secret and raise him on my own.' A tear slid down her cheek, and finally her wet eyes lifted to his face. 'I'm so sorry for what I did to you—to you both.'

'Don't.' His voice rumbled from the depths of his soul. 'Don't apologise to me. I blamed you when I first found out, but how can I blame you now?'

He moved closer, needing to comfort her the only way he knew how. He brushed his lips over hers and felt her shuddering breath as she exhaled. 'I'm the one who's been in the wrong. I was wrong to go to you that night, wrong to push you away so hard afterwards, saying whatever I needed to make you realise how wrong I was for you. I was wrong not to contact you afterwards. You weren't a child, but you were so much younger than me, and considerably less worldly.' His hands splayed over her cheeks, drawing her closer, his lips on hers now. 'I'm sorry.'

She sobbed. He caught her anguish with his mouth, then he kissed her, slowly at first, gently, his mouth apologising to her. But then her small groan ignited something deep in his soul so, without his intention, his kiss deepened, conveying urgency and need, his hands moving to her hips, lifting her to sit on the edge of the bench, his hands curving over her bottom, holding her pressed to arousal, his kiss a demand and a promise. The spark that had ignited between them earlier that morning had caused a full-blown explosion now.

He continued to kiss her as his hands began to roam her body, and hers did likewise, pushing at his shirt, her fingers working the buttons slowly but determinedly, undoing the top two before she made a sound of frustration and simply lifted it from the waistband of his trousers. Her fingertips explored the muscular ridges of his abdomen, following the lines there until she reached his hair-roughened nipples and touched them so tentatively, he wanted to let out a guttural oath.

It was like the breaking of a dam, the beating of a drum that couldn't be contained. He lifted her from the bench, wrapping her legs around his waist, carrying her from the kitchen without breaking their kiss, and her hands continued to roam his body hungrily, each touch like a promise of what was to come. He needed her in a way that made no sense, yet it also made all the sense in the world.

She pushed at his shirt as they entered his study. He was rarely in Sydney so the space, while beautiful, was devoid of the clutter in his Singapore office. He carried her to the large white sofa, laying her down and following after her, his body weight on hers, his kiss dominating her as his hands found the hem of her dress and pushed it upwards, just as he'd wanted to do when she'd shown it to him on the rack. He'd imagined her wearing it, imagined himself removing it. A heady rush of achievement flooded his body.

This would be the silver lining to their marriage—the one thing they could build a relationship around. He pushed at the dress, lifting away to remove it from her completely, and then he stopped. He didn't kiss her again, even though he wanted to, because there was something he wanted to do so much more desperately.

He wanted to look at her. To see her. See the body he hadn't been in the right frame of mind to fully appreciate the night they'd made love, yet still remembered well enough to see the changes made by a child, a few years. Despite her slim frame, her breasts had grown rounder, her hips too. He cupped her breasts possessively, as though he had every right, as though she were his in every way, his mouth finding hers once more, his fingers teasing her nipples, making her arch her back and moan in a way he understood on a primal level.

'Yes,' he promised, though she hadn't said anything. She didn't need to. 'Soon.'

Her fingertips stilled for a moment, then gained momentum, moving up his back, dragging down, her nails pushing into the waistband of his trousers and curving into the top of his bottom, dragging him closer to her, lifting her hips at the same time, as though trying to unite them.

'Too many clothes,' she said breathlessly. It

was a sentiment with which he one hundred per cent concurred.

'Way too many.'

He pushed to standing, his eyes burning into hers as he stripped himself of fabric completely before dispensing with her underwear. Once again, he could only look—the sight of her was so intoxicating, like a drug he'd never known he was craving. The curls of hair at the top of her thighs, the fullness of her breasts, their creamy skin and the pinkness of her nipples. She had matured into a woman's body, and he wanted, more than anything, to make her his.

A voice in the back of his mind was shouting at him, reminding him he'd already acted on his own selfish impulses where Annabelle was concerned, taking her because it had suited him, regardless of what had been right for her. But this was different, wasn't it? They were getting married. They already had a child together.

His arousal was straining so hard, it was painful; he could feel heat building up inside him, begging to be released.

Any woman would have done.

That wasn't true. He'd needed Annabelle that night, just as he needed her now. He didn't know why she had this power over him, but she did. That didn't absolve him of his obligations, though, his duty to do the right thing by her. If anything, it made it so much more imperative that he did so.

She wasn't just the mother of his child, she was still Lewis's sister, and he owed them all more than just the animalistic indulgence of his urges.

'Please,' she whimpered, her fingertips moving to her breasts, cupping them so he swore under his breath, the temptation almost too much to bear.

'God, Annabelle, I want this.'

'Me too.' She pushed up to sitting, reaching for his hand and yanking him back to the sofa. He went even when he knew he should have fought her. He sat and she lifted herself up to straddle him, her cheeks pink, her eyes fevered.

'But we can't do this,' he muttered, shaking his head in disbelief at what he was saying. His arousal begged him to reconsider.

'What?' she murmured, as though she'd misheard him. Her hand dropped between them, cupping his masculine strength, the pad of her thumb brushing over his tip. He dropped his head back, his eyes squeezed shut as a bead of moisture escaped.

'We should wait. Until we're married.'

'What?' This time it was higher-pitched, rife with disbelief. 'You have got to be kidding me.'

Her beautiful body jack-knifed off him, her eyes showing surprise, then hurt.

He stood, moving towards her, but she lifted a hand, stilling him. 'Don't. Just let me… You're saying you don't want to sleep with me?'

And, despite the seriousness of that moment, his lips curved in a sardonic smile. 'Does that look like what I'm saying?' He gestured to his rampant erection, and felt a flood of warmth at the innocent blush that spread over her cheeks.

'Annabelle, seven years ago I made a selfish decision that has completely changed your life. If we have sex right now, I have no reason to think you're not going to regret it, and that you're not going to think I've taken advantage of you.'

'But—you're the one who said you want this to be a real marriage.'

He rubbed his hand over his stubbly jaw. 'I do want that. I want us to find some common ground, and right now the fact we obviously still have this chemistry is a great start. But you're completely blindsided by all this—I'm not going to take advantage of you in what could just be a moment of indecision or uncertainty.' He ignored her lifted hand, moving closer, so he could lace his fingers with hers.

'I want you. I want you more than I have words to express, so believe me when I say it's taking all my willpower to walk away from you. But it's what I should have done seven years ago.'

Her eyes were huge, hollowed out. 'You regret it that much?'

He shifted his head, surprised by her interpretation. But it was accurate. 'Yes,' he said with a nod. 'I do. Not because that night wasn't great. Not because I didn't want you. But because I should have been strong enough to understand that we weren't well-matched. You were nothing like the women I usually see. You still aren't.'

She spun away from him, dragging her hand free. Her back was trembling.

'I know that.'

'No, you still don't understand. You're so beautiful, Annabelle, but you're also so innocent. So inexperienced and naïve. For me, that night was just sex, and for you it was…what? Love?'

He saw her flinch. 'Whatever I thought it was then doesn't matter now.'

'But it does. If we're going to have a physical relationship, we need to define the parameters of that first. I won't hurt you again, Annabelle. I have regretted hurting you for seven years—I can't remember that night without a deep sense of shame. I won't let that happen again.'

She'd turned back around and was staring at him as though he'd just said, 'I kill kittens for fun.'

How could she not see what he was doing? That this was a sacrifice and a half? Did she have any idea how much his body was scream-ing for her?

'Seven years ago, I thought you cared for me,' she whispered, and that same sense of shame and guilt fired inside him once more. 'I was stupid and naïve, just like you said.'

'I did care for you, Annabelle.'

She rejected that. 'You cared about Lewis's sister, not about me as my own person.'

'I cared about you enough to push you away—hard—so you wouldn't waste any more of your time fantasising about me.'

She held up a hand again to silence him. 'I'd

built you up in my mind to be something you weren't. I had all these ideas about you, and I know it was stupid. It was a crush. I don't feel any of those things now.'

He wondered why that bothered him so much. Ego, he thought, with a shake of his head.

'I've had seven years to wake up and smell the coffee. I get it. I was just someone for you to have sex with, nothing more meaningful. You're someone who lives your life in a certain way. I don't have any problem with that, and you shouldn't feel bad about it. My expectations were just way out of step with the reality of what you were offering. But they're not now. I get what the parameters of this are. I get that sex is probably the only thing we'll ever have in common.'

'And that's enough for you?' he asked, carefully keeping his voice devoid of emotion.

She sighed. It was all he needed to hear. He moved closer, coming to stand in front of her.

'I'm not going anywhere.' He lifted his hand to her arm, slowly running a finger down it, his gaze following the gesture, noting the goose bumps that followed in its wake. 'Let's take it slow and make sure you don't get hurt this time around. Okay?'

CHAPTER SIX

ANNIE RAN HER fingers over the rows and rows of designer outfits, shaking her head as she moved around the walk-in wardrobe. Could it still be called a wardrobe when it was the size of her old apartment? she mused, pulling a drawer open and gasping when she saw that it was filled with neatly organised handbags—also boasting designer names. She shut it again quickly.

This couldn't all be for her, surely?

Everything she'd tried on that morning and loved was there, but there was much more as well. It was as though someone had taken her impressions and used them as the building blocks of her fantasy wardrobe. There was everything from casual—jeans and yoga pants—to sophisticated and glamorous—slinky silken dresses, and even a couple of ball gowns, as well as trouser suits and blouses. It was the kind of wardrobe a teenaged Annie would have fantasised about.

With a small smile, she pulled one of the

dresses up and held it against herself. Just as in the boutique, she saw how beautiful the dress was, and how much it suited her. She imagined that when she wore it she would look, and feel, a million dollars.

Speaking of which, all the price tags had been removed, which was a saving grace, because if she could easily tally up what he'd spent she'd *never* let him keep them. That, though, was a technicality. She could estimate the expense and it didn't change the fact that her heart had lifted at the sight of so many beautiful things, and all for her.

Ordinarily, she might have gone to lightly chastise him, and then to thank him, but what had happened between them earlier had caused Annie anxiety all evening. Max had arrived home not long after Dimitrios had put an end to their passion so she'd been able to busy herself with the important job of helping him assimilate this dramatic change in his circumstances. Fortunately, Max was a grounded kid and—mostly— he took it on the chin. His room was enormous, and he found the idea of a nanny interesting, but having his familiar books and train set waiting for him in his room seemed to assuage any concerns he might have had.

They had dinner together—burgers that Dimitrios ordered in, which Max ate with gusto, earning many beaming smiles of pride from Dimitrios. Annie had watched their interactions with a sense of sadness—at what the two had lost because of her—and pleasure—because it clearly wasn't too late for them to build a meaningful relationship.

That was why they were doing this and, whatever personal sacrifice that required Dimitrios and her to make, it was completely worth it.

As for their own personal relationship, maybe he was right. Maybe they shouldn't rush into bed together. A day ago, Annie would have laughed off the suggestion, but Dimitrios's appeal was as magnetic as ever. She was going to have to work extremely hard to fight it.

But did she even want to?

I don't want you to get hurt again.

Once she skipped over the mortification of how much of her heart was being worn on her sleeve, his thoughtfulness was pretty reassuring. She'd been a teenager the last time they'd had sex, and he *had* hurt her. By design! He'd aimed to break whatever illusions and hopes she'd built up thanks to one night of passionate sex. He'd said what he needed to—the harshest things he could think of—to push her away. It had worked. She'd been devastated, and furious, but he was doing everything he could to avoid her going through that again.

She could have told him he needn't have worried. His diatribe that night had spawned something new in Annie; she was no longer the person she'd been then. She'd never be that woman again.

The fact he'd been her only lover didn't change how she viewed sex now—it was purely a physical act. It didn't mean anything. Just because they desired each other didn't mean their feelings were—or ever had to be—involved. It was only passion. Respect and friendship had to be worked on separately.

And what about love? a little voice inside her demanded. *What about the fairy stories and the idea of a happily ever after?*

Childish nonsense, Annie thought, pushing that little voice deep inside her as she walked back through the bedroom and into the hallway.

She was looking for Dimitrios, to thank him

for the clothes. What she hadn't expected to find was him in their son's room. She checked her watch; it was half an hour after Max's bed time. Dimitrios had said he'd tuck him in and, given how much he'd missed, and the fact Max had seemed fine with it, Annie hadn't objected. She slowed down as she approached the door, the deep rumble of Dimitrios's voice setting goose bumps along her arms.

'This one is from when I was a boy, not much older than you.'

'What happened?'

She wanted to peer round the door to see what Dimitrios was talking about, but she knew then that they might see her and stop talking.

'My brother—your uncle Zach—you'll like him.' She could hear the smile in Dimitrios's voice. 'He liked to go to the Rocks, just down there.' Annie closed her eyes, picturing Sydney's famous Rocks area. 'There's an old bridge and a set of steps. We used to climb half way up them and then jump down, pretending we could fly.'

His laugh filled Annie's tummy with butter-flies.

'Really?'

'Mmm,' he said. 'But we couldn't fly, as it turns

out. I got this scar when I fell and hit my arm on the footpath. My mother wasn't very pleased.'

There was silence and she tried to imagine what the expression on Max's little face would be like. Eventually, frustrated, she moved just a little, shifting to peer round the door. Her heart cracked wide open. Dimitrios was propped up on the bed beside Max, his large frame just a grown-up version of Max's. Max had his left arm out and she presumed the one scar he bore—from when he'd fallen off his scooter as a two-year-old—had been the initial subject of the conversation.

'Is that my grandma?'

'Yes,' Dimitrios confirmed, his voice neutral.

'Where does she live?'

'Right here in Sydney.'

'How come I've never met her?'

Dimitrios looked around the room; Annie shifted backward, out of sight.

'You'll meet her soon. At the wedding.'

'Does she live with you?'

'No. I live in Singapore, remember?'

'Oh, yes.' Max tilted his head to the side, lost in thought. 'I'd miss my mummy if she ever didn't live in the same house as me.'

Perhaps some sixth sense alerted Dimitrios to her presence, because at that exact moment he lifted his gaze and pinpointed her immediately, his eyes latching on to hers.

'You won't have to worry about that.' His lips curved in a small smile; she found herself returning it. 'You're going to be stuck with your mummy and me for a very long time.'

She moved a step backward, into the hallway, tears stinging her eyes. He'd said that he didn't want to hear about their son from her. He wanted to get to know Max all on his own. She was watching that happen and it was an act of beauty and magic.

'Now.' She heard the natural authority in Dimitrios's voice, even when it was softened by affection. 'It's far later than I realised. You must get to sleep, Max.'

Right on cue, Max yawned. 'Okay, Dimitrios.'

Her heart twisted. Soon, that would change to Daddy.

At the door, Dimitrios emerged, his eyes finding Annie's. But Max called out, 'Wait! You forgot to tell me about the one on your chin.'

Annie watched as Dimitrios lifted a finger and pressed it to a small scar that ran along the ridge of his jaw line. It wasn't a new scar; she remembered it from the night they'd... She couldn't think of that. Her body was still tingling from the kisses and touches they'd shared earlier today.

'Remind me at breakfast.'

'What will we eat?'

Dimitrios's smile flicked towards Annie, warming her belly. 'What would you like?'

'Pancakes?'

Dimitrios laughed, the sound reaching inside Annie and setting something free.

'How about eggs?' he suggested instead.

Max paused. 'Okay, I guess so.'

Annie was impressed. It would have been easy for him to agree to Max's request for pancakes, but Dimitrios had instinctively known not to indulge Max's every whim, especially not with junk food.

By silent agreement, they moved further down the corridor before speaking. 'You're great with kids,' she said honestly, lifting her face towards his as they walked.

'I have good friends who have children. I've spent some time with them.'

It was a curious thing to contemplate—his life now, what it looked like. They'd known each other years ago. Dimitrios had been twenty-four the last time they'd slept together, and his life-style had probably been quite typical for some-one his age. Now, in his early thirties, what did his social life look like?

'That surprises you?'

She smiled wistfully. 'I guess I had imagined you still going on as you were then. You know, partying and all that. But it's been seven years.'

He stopped walking, his brow furrowed as he looked down at her. 'That was never really my scene, Annabelle. Zach, yes, but for me I gen-erally used to go for a drink then head home to work.'

She lifted her shoulders, indicating it didn't really matter, but in contradiction to that heard herself ask, 'Is that really true?'

'Why would I lie to you?'

'You wouldn't,' she said instantly. 'It's just the papers…'

'Yes, I know. Zach and I are tabloid fodder.'

'As am I now, apparently.' She chewed on her lower lip, thinking of the mortifying article that had run the day before. She stopped walking, lifting a hand to his arm to stop him. 'That's why you took me shopping this morning, isn't it? Because of that piece about me being dowdy and unsophisticated?'

A muscle jerked in his jaw and he looked as though he was quite capable of strangling a bear with his bare hands. 'I didn't know you'd seen it.'

'Yeah, a friend emailed it to me.'

He was studying her thoughtfully, his eyes roaming her face. 'You're not upset?'

She shrugged. 'I mean, it wasn't the nicest thing I've ever read, but it's not like I'm under any illusions here. I know what I am, and what you are. That article's probably been the closest to the truth since our "whirlwind romance" was announced.'

That caused his frown to deepen.

'You're not dowdy.'

'Well, I'm probably not now, after your whole Cinderella treatment today,' she said with a small laugh, and began to walk again, but it was Dimitrios who caught her wrist this time, holding her still.

'You never were. I didn't arrange that because I thought you needed to change.'

She lifted a brow, his denial unexpected. 'No? So why did you?'

He lifted a hand as though to cup her cheek

but dropped it again. 'Your poverty made you an easy target. I didn't like to see you being bullied like that. I don't like to think of Max hearing that kind of thing said about his mother.'

Ah, Max. Of course. All good deeds came back to Max—just as they should. And, though he hadn't referred to Lewis, she was sure that promise was there too—a desire to look after her simply because she was Lewis's sister.

She smiled again but this time it felt a little brittle. 'Well, thank you. I didn't expect to find a wardrobe the size of my old apartment here, nor that it would be stocked with such incredible clothes. It was very generous of you.'

His eyes wouldn't shift, though. They stayed locked to hers so swirls of emotion spun through her belly.

'It wasn't generous, so much as appropriate. You must start thinking of yourself as my wife— all that I have is yours.'

'For as long as we're married,' she couldn't help quipping, but she said it with a wink, to show she was joking. 'And thank you again. It's going to take me some time to get used to that. Actually, I'm not sure I'll ever get used to that, but I do appreciate you trying to make me feel comfortable in this palace.' She gestured around them, her eyes following the lines of the room. 'It's just—' she added and then stopped.

He put a hand on the small of her back, guiding her deeper into the lounge and across it, to where a bar was set up.

'Yes?' he prompted as he opened a decanter containing an amber liquid and poured two measures, handing one to her. She expected the fragrance to be an assault but it had a honey-like quality that was gentle.

'A week ago, I was furiously budgeting to work out how I could get Max what he wants for Christmas.' Her voice was rueful. 'I know that must seem strange to you, but it's why the last few months have been so tough. He's such a smart kid and I don't want him to miss out on stuff because I can't—couldn't—provide him with the material things a lot of his friends have.' She lifted her slender shoulders in a shrug. 'It's not as though he'd asked for anything extravagant, but for me even normal things are hard to afford. So, yeah, this is going to take some getting used to.'

'What did he ask for for Christmas?'

'A remote-controlled car and a train for his

tracks that has a motor, so he can set it going and watch it travel in circles.' She smiled indulgently. 'What can I say? He's an automobile kind of kid.'

Dimitrios's eyes glowed with something she didn't understand. 'You don't need to worry about anything like that ever again. Whatever you think he should have, consider it done.'

'But I don't want him to be spoiled,' she said quickly.

'No.' Dimitrios sipped his drink then gestured towards the deck. It was a beautiful night, the stars twinkling above Sydney, the Opera House gleaming like a pearl in the moonlight.

She walked beside him, wondering at the surreal nature of this. Why did it feel so natural for them to be together like this? There was a level of comfort between them that she hadn't been prepared for.

'What is Christmas usually like, for you and Max?' Dimitrios prompted conversationally, guiding her to a bench seat that overlooked the view.

'Quiet,' she said thoughtfully. 'We go to church in the morning, then come home and Max opens his presents. I can usually pull together enough to buy him two or three—just small things. Mum and Dad send something—though it's usually practical, like clothes, because they know he's growing like a weed.' She breathed out so her side-swept fringe shifted, catching the moon's golden light across her hair. 'I make something special for lunch, something we don't have any other time of year—salmon or turkey—and then we watch a movie and have a little piece of pudding each. Pretty normal.'

Then, with a smile, she turned to face him, crossing one leg over the other. 'Though, I suppose "normal" is a very relative term. Your Christmases are probably very different to mine.'

He smiled, but it was constrained. 'Actually, our Christmases are usually quiet too. Zach hates Christmas—always has, probably always will. And Mum has her step-kids, who make a huge fuss of her, so she generally lets us skate by without expecting us to visit or anything.'

Nerves spread through Annie like wildfire. Somehow, for some reason, she'd thought of Dimitrios as existing in some kind of void. She hadn't followed through the idea that, by keeping Max from Dimitrios, she was also keeping him from Zach and their mother, and any other family members who might feel that they wanted to get to know Dimitrios's son.

'Is she angry about me keeping her grandson from her?'

Dimitrios took a sip of his drink. 'No.'

Annie found herself leaning closer, though she'd heard him fine. 'How can she not be? After what you've lost, and what she's lost?'

'Because I'm marrying you, and she knows better than to complain to me about my choice of bride.'

'Ah.' Annie's smile was instinctive. 'So she's afraid of you?'

Dimitrios shook his head firmly. 'Not at all. She knows that once I've made a decision I'll stick to it, come hell or high water. What would the point be in questioning me, or you?'

'That doesn't mean she's not angry.'

'Would you feel better if she were?'

Annie considered that. 'In a way, yes.'

'Why?'

'Because I think I probably deserve it.'

Dimitrios stared at her for several seconds, his eyes showing a hint of frustration but his voice was gentle.

'You tried to tell me about him. And, since

then, you have sacrificed everything to raise our child. I wish things between us had been different but, after the way I treated you, I have only myself to blame.'

'You're being so understanding...'

'I'm not an ogre.' He frowned. 'Though I can see why you might think I was.'

'You *were* pretty brutal that night.'

He dipped his head forward in silent agreement.

'I can't believe we're getting married in two days.'

He turned to face her thoughtfully. 'You can't believe it as in, it's not what you want?'

She considered that, lifting her shoulders. She remembered the way he'd been with Max, and the things Max had said about wanting to live with his mother for ever, and she found herself shaking her head. 'I think we're doing the right thing. Max is worth it.'

His eyes held Annie's for several seconds and then he nodded. 'Yes. He is.'

CHAPTER SEVEN

'YOU'RE NERVOUS.'

Her eyes lifted from her lap to his face, then shifted to the window behind him, and the view that sped past as the car moved. Her fingers were clasped in her lap, her features drawn. Annabelle Papandreo looked beautiful, wealthy and untouchable. Her blonde hair had been clipped to one side, and for their wedding she'd worn a stunningly ornate headband that invoked a nineteen-forties vibe. Her gown had been similarly timeless, art nouveau lace meeting silk, hugging her body all the way to the floor.

'Is that silly?' she asked.

He shook his head, finding it hard to look away from her face. Some time after boarding the flight, she'd taken all her make-up off and slipped into a change of clothes, far less glamorous than the wedding outfit but every bit as striking—a black linen singlet paired with a pair of silk trousers.

Dimitrios had found the flight a unique torment, his fingers itching to reach out and feel the different textures for himself.

'It's just been a big day,' she pointed out, referring to the whirlwind of their brief morning ceremony, the lunch with his family and a few select friends—only those he thought she'd like best—and then the flight to Singapore.

The moment they'd stepped off his private jet and on to the tarmac, the sultry night heat had wrapped around them. Max hadn't seemed to notice, nor mind, but Annabelle had fanned her face with a magazine as they'd walked, then turned the air-conditioning up in the limousine as soon as they were inside. It was like an ice cube now, but again, Max was impervious to the climate—he was fast asleep in his car seat, opposite them.

'You did very well.'

She spun back to face him, her eyes scanning his face for sincerity. How could she doubt his words? It had been a big day, just as she'd said, yet in every way she'd carried herself with pride and grace. He had known she was nervous about seeing his brother and meeting his mother and yet she'd embraced them, taking time to speak to them at length, showing them who she was and making inroads into forming a genuine relationship with both of them.

There was nothing about her that had seemed unhappy, or had spoken of the unusual terms of their marriage. To anyone watching, they would have seemed like a perfectly normal couple on their wedding day.

If Zach thought Dimitrios's about-face with regard to marriage was strange, he'd had the manners not to say as much on Dimitrios's wedding day. But Dimitrios had decided a long time ago that he wasn't interested in love or marriage—he'd seen what 'love' had done to his mother and it had been a salutary example of what he never wanted to become.

Which was why this marriage was so damned perfect.

As he'd advanced in years, one part of his plan hadn't sat well for Dimitrios—the lack of children. He'd felt a yearning to continue his lineage, but he'd still been reconciled to not having that, given that he didn't want a traditional marriage.

And here Annabelle had presented him with all the pieces of a marriage he wanted—if he could have cherry-picked the perfect situation, it would be exactly this. He desired her, he respected her and she'd already borne him a son, so it was likely they'd have more children when they were ready. Yeah, he was feeling pretty damned good about things—especially because he'd also taken great pains to make sure he was looking after her feelings this time round.

Relaxed, he stretched an arm along the back of the leather car-seat, his fingers dangling tantalisingly close to the exposed skin of her shoulder.

'So what are you nervous about?'

Her brow furrowed, her eyelashes sweeping down and hiding her expression for a moment. She had a little dimple in her cheek that deepened when she frowned and pursed her lips like that. Out of nowhere, he imagined leaning forward and pressing his tongue to it.

Later.

'I mean...' She darted a glance at him and then looked down, twirling her engagement ring around her finger. He'd already spotted that habit she'd developed. 'This ring, the private jet, now a limousine...and I can't help noticing that these houses are kind of enormous.' She gestured to Ocean Drive as they moved round it.

'You've already seen a photo of my house.'

'I know. It's just hitting me that this is where we live now.'

'You'll get used to it.'

'What if I don't?'

'Then we'll move back to Sydney.' The quickness of his response surprised him—his willingness to leave the life he had here was something he hadn't known he felt. Then again, he'd expected Annabelle to simply pick up and leave her life, and all that was familiar to her. Why should it be any different for him?

'I think a big part of it is making sure Max settles in well. So long as he's happy at school, then I'm sure I'll be happy.'

He heard the determination in her voice and admired her for it. She really wanted to make a success of this.

'When did you move here?' she asked a little uneasily as the car turned into the section of road that led to his home.

'Four years ago.'

'Right, you said that.' Her tongue darted out, licking her lower lip. 'Why Singapore?'

'We spent a lot of time here—our teenage years. It feels as much my home as Australia. And then, a few years back, we expanded into a television network and a masthead of magazines and newspapers. I moved here first, but Zach spends around half his time here now too—we both love it, to be honest. It's a convenient springboard to anywhere in the world.'

That made a lot of sense. 'It was good to see Zach again. He hasn't changed.'

'No.' Dimitrios laughed, but there was a hint of worry at the back of that laugh, a worry he generally didn't express to anyone. Yet, despite that, he found himself saying, 'To be honest, when that journalist sent me a photo of Max, my first thought was that Zach must be the father.'

It seemed to distract Annabelle from her anxiety. Her eyes moved to Max and a small smile curved her lips. The first since they'd boarded the jet, he realised.

'Why?'

'Well, he bears more than a passing resemblance.' Dimitrios tried to make light of his admission, but Annie shook her head.

'Well, you *are* twins,' she responded in a droll tone.

Dimitrios nodded.

'So why, then?'

'Let's just say the rumours about me are generally exaggerated.'

'You mean you don't go through women like most men go through underwear?' she prompted, and though her voice was calm she was watching him with an intensity that told him to be careful—he didn't want to give her false hope about him.

'I'm not a saint,' he said with a lift of his shoulders. 'I've been with women. But I'm careful. You are the only woman I've ever lost control with.'

She looked towards Max, perhaps double-checking he was still asleep.

He moved the subject off himself. 'Zach is more...carefree. We're twins, yes, but we're very different. If either of us was going to accidentally get a woman pregnant, I would have put money on it being him.'

Annabelle tilted her head to one side, considering that, but whatever response she was about to offer, it wasn't to be. Her attention was caught by something behind him, and her lips parted, so he turned to see his house from her perspective. The size of it was impressive but it was more than that. The car paused at enormous gates that swung open on their approach, then it swept up a long drive, past ancient trees with huge canopies that provided much-needed shade on summer days.

'This is it, then,' she said, but quietly, more to herself than him. He wanted to wipe the worry from her face, to give her courage, so before he could second-guess the wisdom of his intentions he leaned forward and pressed a kiss to her lips. It was only meant to be brief, just a boost of strength, a distraction, but the second their lips connected he felt a surge of adrenaline coursing through his veins. His body moved closer, pressing hers back against the car, kissing her until her hands lifted and tangled in the collar of his shirt and she made that sweet little moan of hers. He swallowed it deep inside himself, thinking how addictive her noises were, how much he liked hearing her make them, how she was unlike any woman he'd ever known.

And she was—because Annabelle was now his wife. Mrs Papandreo.

The door to the limousine opened. He fought a wave of frustration at the interruption. What had he been hoping for? To have his way with her here in the back seat of the car? Their son was asleep only a short distance away. Where the hell had his self-control gone?

'What was that for?' Her eyes were enormous, her lower lip full and dark from the pressure of his kiss.

'To distract you,' he said. 'Did it work?'

She shifted, casting a glance towards the house then turned back to face him. 'For about three seconds.'

And, despite the fact he was the one who'd called a halt to the physical side of their relationship, he found himself saying, 'I might have to be more inventive, then.'

Her intake of breath was audible. He smiled, loving how easily he could arouse her, tease her—but that wasn't a one-way street. When he stepped out of the limousine behind Annabelle, he was conscious of how badly he wanted her.

'Max is exhausted,' she observed, the nervousness back in her voice.

'There's been a lot going on recently.'

'Yes. And he was so excited to be on the plane, he barely slept.'

He'd noticed that. Max's curiosity had been insatiable. He'd wanted to understand everything he could about planes—the atmosphere, engines, jet fuel, air traffic control. Dimitrios had answered all the questions he himself would have had as a boy, but he knew there'd be still more to follow from Max.

'He's very intelligent,' Dimitrios murmured.

'Yes. There was some talk of putting him up a year, but I decided to hold him where he is for now.'

Dimitrios straightened, midway to reaching into the car. 'Why?'

'You don't agree with my decision?'

'That's not what I said. I'm just curious. I would have thought most people would be thrilled by the possibility of that.'

'Not me. I know he's a smart kid. He'll do great things as he gets older. But he has to develop socially too, and putting him up an academic year or two could be really hard for him to juggle. He's happy—he was happy—with his peers. I thought I'd see how he was doing in a few years and then decide if it's worth considering.'

Dimitrios reached into the car to unbuckle Max, lifting him easily and carrying him over one shoulder. 'I'll get Max into bed and then show you around.'

* * *

Her head was spinning so fast, it truly felt as though it might come off altogether. She'd seen the outside of his house and she'd seen his penthouse in Sydney so she'd known to expect grand. But this was a whole new level of grand. While the house was some kind of brilliant tribute to modernism, with the appearance of concrete cubes all stuck together to form different spaces—including several rooms that seemed to be both outdoor and indoor at the same time—it also boasted an incredible array of antiques, all Singaporean, ancient and fascinating.

She found herself wanting to ask question upon question about each one, but instead contented herself with admiring them from a distance— a sculpture here, a fountain there, a tapestry, a vase. The ceilings were high, the floors marble and tile, polished to a high sheen. In the background there was an army of servants, all wearing black uniforms, the women in white aprons, moving silently and almost unseen—except Annie *did* see them. She saw everything—with a mixed sense of awe and fascination.

It was hot, too—far hotter than in Sydney— though inside was blessedly air-conditioned.

She looked around the room he'd brought her to. It was technically their bedroom, but it was so much more. At least four times the size of her apartment, it boasted a bed carved from wood, large and ornate, and a sofa that was covered in velvet, a beautiful shade of apple-green. The floors were timber with a large brightly coloured rug, and wooden French doors opened out on to a balcony. Curtains billowed from it.

Fascinated, Annie moved in that direction, aware of Dimitrios's eyes following her progress, and then his body walking behind hers. The steamy heat hit her like a wall when she emerged, but she breathed in deeply, the air inexplicably tropical. Her hands curved around the railing as she took in the new, unfamiliar skyline. Lights shone brightly in one direction, including the Marina Bay towers she'd seen on television. In the other, it was sheer darkness.

'The bay,' he explained, pointing from behind her, so his arm brushed hers. 'In the morning, you'll see it for yourself. It's beautiful.'

She shifted her face a little, looking up at him. It was a mistake. He was closer than she'd realised and in moving she'd brought her lips within reach of his cheek. The compulsion to press forward and kiss him was overpowering.

Our marriage won't be based on love, but it can still be good.

Everything about this whirlwind was like a fairy story, except for that. Annie and Dimitrios knew what no one looking in from the outside could see. It was all fake. The vows they'd spoken to one another, promising to love and honour, were a lie. A lie born out of love—but love for Max, and even Lewis, not for each other.

She sighed, looking away from Dimitrios, focussing on the towers across the water. 'They're beautiful.' Her voice was hoarse, and she swallowed to moisten her mouth. 'I've seen them in movies, but in real life, they're huge.'

Had he moved even closer? In the sultry night air, she caught a hint of his masculine aroma, and her stomach clenched in automatic response.

'An excellent spot for Christmas shopping.'

She wrinkled her nose, well aware that the shops in a building such as that were bound to be incredibly high-end.

'I see your hesitation, Mrs Papandreo,' he said quietly, the words a caress against her ear. Her pulse lifted. She felt an ache deep inside, a need to push backward a little and lean against his broad chest, to feel his closeness and have his arms wrap around her. She wanted to pretend, just for one night, that their marriage was a *real* marriage. That this was a normal wedding night, and the passion that flowed between them had roots in love, as well as lust.

But Annie knew the risks inherent in such pretence. She had to stay on her toes.

'Perhaps,' she said with a little lift of her shoulders. 'I didn't see a Christmas tree in your house.'

Dimitrios stayed close and she was glad of that. 'It's still three weeks away.'

Annie turned to face him then. 'That's soon.'

'Then I'll have a tree brought in.'

'Do you have decorations?'

'They'll bring those too.'

She shook her head, a smile tickling her lips. 'Life really is different for you.'

'Is that a complaint?'

'On the contrary. I'm starting to think I could get used to this.'

'We're so high up, Mummy! I feel like I could fly.'

'Don't you dare. Don't even think about it.' She

reached out and grabbed Max by the back of his shirt, her heart rate accelerating at the very idea of him pitching his little body over the railing.

Dimitrios laughed, leaning closer so he could whisper in her ear. 'I don't really think he's going to jump, do you?'

Embarrassed, she threw him a look. 'We're so high up.'

'And perfectly safe.' He nudged her shoulder then reached down, taking Max's hand in his. 'Now, no more giving your mother a heart attack.' He winked at Annie and began to walk off, the two of them so similar that she stood where she was for a moment, high above Singapore, enjoying the vista of the Supertrees and the walkway that linked two of them. The view was incomparable, the air cool and fresh up there. And, more than that, Max was in seventh heaven after a whole day spent exploring Bay South with Dimitrios.

The sun was lowering in the sky, casting the world in shades of orange, and a moment later Dimitrios slowed to a stop and turned back towards Annie.

'You coming?' he mouthed, their eyes sparking even at this distance.

She swallowed and began to move, catching them easily. Dimitrios reached for her hand and she let him, the sense of rightness spreading through her as they walked.

'This is like magic.' Max's voice was filled with wonder. Annie couldn't disagree.

'You should see it at night.' Dimitrios gestured to the Supertrees that made up this man-made grove. 'The trees light up like big sparklers.'

Max's face showed suitable awe.

'It sounds breath-taking,' Annie murmured. Dimitrios stopped walking and stared at her. His look was so full of admiration and intensity that her heart warmed, her cheeks turned pink and she felt a thousand and one things.

He lifted a hand, brushing his thumb across her cheek, and then he smiled, a smile that reached right inside her and made her feel special and perfect.

'What's that, down there?'

Annie followed Max's gaze. 'It looks like some kind of street performance. A magic show, perhaps?' Nestled amongst the trees on street level, a group had set up, and a crowd had formed to watch them.

'Cool! Magic! Can we go see?'

Annie had been about to distract him, but Dimitrios spoke first. 'Sure, buddy. It's on the way home.'

Home. Her heart shifted gear; she did her best to tame it into submission.

Hours later, a weary Max was carried through the doors of their house by his father. Annie was too alive to feel weary. The day had been one of the best of her life. A spontaneous suggestion to show Max some sights had led to a picnic lunch by the water, and an afternoon spent at the Gardens by the Bay, the skywalk and then finally a pleasurable hour watching talented magicians wow their crowd.

'He's exhausted,' she murmured as they approached the door. Dimitrios ruefully caught her eye over Max's head.

'Perhaps I pushed it too far today.'

'No,' she denied. She'd never forget the sight of Max and his dad playing soccer together— such a simple act, but one that had spoken of love and togetherness, something she hoped to see repeated often. 'It was perfect.'

Their eyes held and her heart sparked once more, rioting in her chest.

'I must admit, I had an ulterior motive in keeping you out so late.'

Annie frowned. 'You did? What?'

'What's an ulterior motive?' Max mumbled sleepily.

Dimitrios pushed the doors open and stood back to allow Annie to enter ahead of him. She did so and then froze...the decorations almost too enormous and over-the-top to process.

'Oh, my goodness. What have you done?'

She whirled around to find Dimitrios watching her carefully.

'Do you like it?'

His question was casual but his voice was deep.

Her expression was lightly mocking. 'No, I hate it.' She pushed lightly at his arm. 'It's incredible.'

He put an arm around her, drawing her close to his side. Magic and mistletoe were so thick in the air, she had to work to remind herself that this was all just pretend. All of it except how much they both loved Max, who was rubbing his bleary eyes and no doubt trying to understand why his father's house now resembled a department store. It had been completely decked out with Christmas finery—all while they'd been out for the day.

'Why?'

'You wanted a Christmas tree.'

'*A* Christmas tree!' she exclaimed with disbelief, lifting a finger. 'As in one. Somewhere. Something small to sit around on Christmas morning and put Max's presents beneath. This is...' She searched for the right word, her eyes saucer-like. 'Spectacular.'

'You deserve spectacular,' he murmured, kissing the tip of her nose, sparking a kaleidoscope of butterflies deep in her tummy. *It's not real.* Somehow, despite all the mistletoe and magic, she *had* to remember that.

CHAPTER EIGHT

'I DIDN'T KNOW *there were butterflies in space.'*

'Hey, who's telling this story?' Lewis pressed a finger to Annie's nose, his wink crinkling one side of his face.

'You.'

'Right, so let me tell it.'

'Keep going.'

'Yes, ma'am. A whole army of butterflies lifted way off the surface of the planet, their wings all silvery and shimmering, so that even in the darkness of space they shone like tiny little stars. Princess Annie put her hand out, like this...' He reached forward and arranged Annie's hand so it was at a funny angle. She giggled. 'And they came to sit on her arm, and her fingertips, and her hair. They were nice butterflies, not the kind that bite you—'

'Butterflies don't bite.'

'Some do.'

'Do not.'

'Annie,' he warned.

She bit down on her lip. 'Okay, keep going.'

'Only two butterflies bit Annie.'

'Hey.' She punched his shoulder.

He grinned.

'They lifted Annie far away from the planet and carried her out into space. The End.'

'Wait a second.' She shook her head. 'That's not a happy ending.'

'Isn't it?'

'No, and you said there's always a happy ending.'

'Ah, so there is.' He stood up from her bed, and Annie wriggled down, arranging her head on the pillow. Lewis pulled the quilt up under her chin, then stroked her head. 'How about this, then? The butterflies carried Princess Annie through space, all the way to her home planet, where she was met with rose petals at her feet and jubilant cries from her adoring public.'

'Better,' she murmured, her eyes heavy.

'She was brought to the palace in a golden carriage, shaped like a pumpkin but with butterfly wings, and there the prince she'd fallen in love with as a child was waiting—he'd never

forgotten her. They got married and lived happily ever after.'

Annie smiled, sleep almost claiming her. 'And the Zap Aliens?'

'They never bothered her again.'

Annie woke with a start, a disorienting confusion seeping into her, so she pushed up and blinked, trying to remember where she was. Not in the small bedroom she'd grown up in, and not with Lewis telling her bed-time stories. Not in her home in Sydney, where she and Max had spent the last six years. Something spiky caught her attention, and then the hint of pine-needle fragrance, and it all came whooshing back.

She lifted her hand to be sure, eyeing the enormous diamond.

Dimitrios. Their marriage. Singapore.

She moved a little, looking at him sleeping, her heart hammering against her ribs. God, what was she doing? Dreams and memories of Lewis had formed a lump in her throat; she stepped out of bed as quietly as she was able, padding gently across the room to the door, which she opened silently, slipping downstairs and into the industrial kitchen.

She silently made a cup of tea and carried it through the downstairs of the sprawling mansion. One of her favourite rooms was a sunken sitting room that seemed to jut out of the house itself. She liked it because there were enormous trees in front of it, so she felt almost as though she were perched in a bird's nest in a rainforest. She pushed the windows wide open and breathed in deeply. It was raining—a heady, tropical rain that smelled of heat, thunder and papaya.

The furniture in this room was dark wood, the cushions colourful. She curled up on a corner of the sofa, cradling the cup in her hands, staring out at the falling rain.

'It's early.' His voice was roughened by sleep. She turned towards the door, bracing herself to see Dimitrios—but nothing could have braced her adequately for the sight of him in only a pair of boxer shorts, his toned, taut abdomen calling for her attention. She looked away quickly.

'I couldn't sleep.'

He walked across the room, taking a seat down the other end of the sofa.

'Did I wake you when I left?'

'Must have.' He shrugged. 'I'm a light sleeper.'

'I'm sorry.'

'Don't be. I like getting up early.'

'This early?'

'Not generally.'

She sipped her tea.

'What woke you?'

There's always a happy ending for you, Annie.

Emotions flooded her. She traced one of the ornate patterns on the rim of the cup, lost in thought.

'I have these dreams.' She sighed. 'More like memories. Of the bed-time stories Lewis used to tell me.'

'What kind of stories?'

Her smile was nostalgic. 'Oh, about dragons and castles and magical caves—stories that would take you to a far-away world or a different star system. There were always monsters and I was the only person who could save the world. I wish he'd written them down—though I'm probably the only one who'd appreciate them.'

Dimitrios was quiet for so long, she shifted to face him.

'You must miss him a lot.'

Annie nodded. 'Yes.' What else could she say? After Lewis died, she'd been completely alone. Her parents hadn't factored. Briefly, there'd been hope—Dimitrios—but whatever comfort she'd gained from their night together had been very, very short-lived.

'Me too.' He tapped his fingertips against his knee, his eyes distant, as though he had travelled back in time. 'He was my best friend. I couldn't believe it when he died.'

'No,' she murmured, taking another sip from her tea. 'It was so sudden—but that was merciful, given how much he hated being sick.'

Dimitrios nodded. 'He had so much potential; what a cruel twist of fate to lose him at only twenty-four years of age. So young.'

'So young,' she agreed.

'I notice Max talks about his Uncle Lewis.'

Annie nodded. 'I've made sure he knows about him. Being an only child, that sibling bond is quite foreign to him.'

Dimitrios reached out, brushing a hand over her hair, then letting it drop to the back of the sofa. 'Would you have liked more children?'

'I always thought I would have more than one,' she said with a little lift of her shoulders. 'I loved being a sister. I liked having someone to tell my secrets to, and Lewis was—a great brother.' She cleared her throat. 'What about you?'

'I never even thought about having children, up until a few years ago.'

'What happened a few years ago?'

'Nothing in particular. Actually, it was hot on the heels of this.' He gestured to their feet. 'Expanding our operations in Singapore. I was on such a high—I felt like Zach and I could do no wrong. We inherited this business that our grandfather built from the ground up, and we've worked so hard to make it bigger and better, but for what? Who's all this for? With no kids, where does it go?'

His fingertips traced an invisible circle on her bare flesh, sending goose bumps along her skin.

'I've never wanted to get married. I've always, always known that about myself.'

Annie's chest felt as though it were being tightened.

'I appreciate how strange that must sound to you—my wife—but our marriage is different. I didn't want to have the emotional pressure of being married. A wife who loved me and needed my love in return.' He grimaced. 'And, as you wisely pointed out, most marriages are based on a presumption of love.'

'Not ours, though,' she said quietly, surprised

her voice sounded so stoic when the admission did something strange to her insides.

'No.' His agreement was swift, his nod a further confirmation of that. 'I didn't want to raise a child as I was raised—going back and forth between a mother and father. So I felt my options were pretty limited. Until I was contacted about Max and everything fell into place.'

A dart of something like resentment moved down her spine. It was all so convenient for Dimitrios. Oh, missing six years of Max's life wasn't ideal, but presumably that was a small price to pay for having a ready-made heir waiting in the wings, and a woman he could draw into exactly the kind of marriage he wanted.

'Why are you so against marriage?' she asked, keeping her voice devoid of emotion.

'Not all marriages,' he quipped with a grin, gesturing from him to her.

'I meant, genuine marriage.'

That lessened his grin, for a moment turning it into a hint of a frown. 'It's not marriage so much as the idea of love,' he said thoughtfully. 'I saw how my dad treated Mum, how he treated us, and I guess it just solidified for me how bad an idea it was to care too much for someone.'

'Why? What happened between them?'

'Nothing. It was a whirlwind affair. She got pregnant. He didn't want kids so he got on with his own life, leaving her in total poverty to raise two boys.'

Annie's stomach turned over. Everything began to fall into place. 'I see.'

His eyes narrowed, and he nodded tightly. 'Yes. Just like I left you.'

Her gaze softened. 'You didn't know.'

'That changes nothing about how much you've been struggling.' His lips tightened with self-condemnation. 'My father saw no intrinsic value in Zach and me until he got married again and my stepmother couldn't have children. She badly wanted them and so he brought us here to Singapore. Our mother was devastated.'

Annie gasped. 'How could he do that to her?'

'He didn't care about her at all,' he said succinctly. 'Theirs was a brief affair and it meant nothing to him. He never thought of her again.'

Annie found it impossible to look at him. She spun her face away, pain wrenching through her, because those exact same words could have applied to her relationship with Dimitrios.

'It's not the same as us,' he said thickly. 'I

have thought of you many, many times since that night, Annabelle.'

Something shifted. Hope. The absence of pain. 'Oh?'

'I pride myself on always being in control. I have never done something I regretted, something I felt happened beyond my control, except for that night with you. After I'd promised Lewis I'd look after you, I did *that*.'

Her eyes swept shut at that admission. 'That's not thinking of me, that's thinking of yourself— and your own perceived failings.'

'It's thinking of you, and wondering what it was about you that drove me over the edge of sanity. Lewis's little sister.' He shook his head. 'What power you held over me.'

A rush of something like pleasure expanded in her chest but she ignored it—there was no power here, no victory. He was talking in the past tense and, even if he hadn't been, it was obvious he resented whatever he thought her source of power was.

'I think it was just shared grief,' she said simply.

'That was definitely a catalyst,' he agreed,

moving closer still. 'But you'd wanted me long before that night.'

Her lips parted at the statement, her cheeks growing pink. 'You looked at me as though you thought I was the second coming. What red-blooded man wouldn't have responded to that?' he asked.

'I was too young to know how to respond to you,' she said with a soft exhalation. 'I'd never met anyone like you.'

'It was a long time ago.' His fingertips found the thin strap of her singlet top and pushed beneath it, his exploration so soft and gentle that it was almost as if he didn't realise he was doing it. 'You're more experienced now.'

Her cheeks glowed with more warmth. 'Am I?'

She didn't need to look at him to know that he was frowning. 'I presume so.'

'More experienced with men?'

'It's been seven years.'

'More than six of which I've spent single-handedly raising a child,' she pointed out, her defensiveness making the words sound more caustic than she'd intended.

'You're saying you haven't been with anyone since me?'

She lifted the cup to her lips, needing a minute. Her brain was going haywire.

'Annabelle?'

God, how she loved that he used her full name. He always had done. She forced herself to look at him, her eyes raking his face. 'You're the only man I've ever been with.'

He flinched a little, clearly shocked by this. 'But it's been seven years.'

'We just discussed that.'

'But you're... How have you gone so long without sex?'

She laughed; she couldn't help it, but sadness flooded her because it was obvious from his response that such an idea was anathema to him. How many women had he been with since her? She didn't want to consider that.

'That night was— I'd been drinking.' He dragged a hand through his hair, moving closer. 'Honestly, I can't even remember if I was as attentive as you deserved. I just know it was your first time and that I hadn't expected that.' He brushed his finger down her arm and she drew in a shuddering breath.

'You were...attentive.'

His hand moved towards her wrist.

'Even drunk, I guess you knew what you were doing. Like you've already said, it didn't matter who you were with, it was just sex.'

His lips compressed. 'I should never have said that.'

'It was the truth, though, right?'

He frowned, his handsome, symmetrical face shifting into something approximating a grimace. 'I needed…a human connection.'

She shifted a little, and her knee brushed his, a thousand sparks shooting through her. 'And I was there.'

He shook his head, lifting a hand to her hair, stroking it. 'You were so brave at the funeral. I was watching you and the way you stood, the way you comforted your parents and were strong for them.' His voice was low and husky and it did something to Annie's insides. 'And all I could think about afterwards was how you must be feeling. Who was comforting you?'

Her heart trembled.

'I'd promised Lewis I'd look after you, but it was more than that. I wanted to make sure you were okay too. But that was all, Annabelle. That's why I went to you. And then you opened the door and a need I couldn't…wouldn't…control overtook me. I have spent the last seven years hating how weak I was in that moment, but maybe it was bigger than weak or strong. Maybe it was just…right.'

Had he moved, or had she? They were closer now, and she breathed in, tasting him on the tip of her tongue. 'It felt right.' It had. Right up until the morning, when he'd left and reality had come crashing down on her.

'You're Lewis's sister.'

She nodded slowly.

'You're the last person I should have gone to, should have slept with.' He groaned. 'You were a virgin, and I was drunk. Everything about it was wrong.'

'No.'

It was a simple answer, straight from her heart.

'It really wasn't.' She put her hand on his knee and he frowned in response. 'Stop torturing yourself for that night. I could have stopped it at any time. I could have pushed you away, told you to wait. I knew you'd been drinking and I knew you were as emotional about Lewis as I was.' She lifted a finger to his lips, silencing anything he might have said in response. 'If either of us was selfish, it was me. I'd had a crush on you for years and I couldn't let you walk away. I took what you offered because I needed it. I wanted you to be my first.'

His eyes flashed with comprehension; something moved deep in their depths.

'But you didn't want to get pregnant,' he growled, still obviously blaming himself.

'No,' she agreed. 'But when I found out I was pregnant I was happy, Dimitrios. The idea of having your child was never a disaster for me. Even when I saw you at the club, and realised it was something I'd probably need to do alone, I was okay.'

'How can that be?'

Her expression was wistful. 'Because I was alone. And so lonely. I never had many friends, and I wasn't close to Mum and Dad. Lewis was… he was my world.'

Dimitrios moved closer, nodding slowly.

'And then you came to me and for one night, one brief, wonderful night, I felt like everything was going to be okay.' She was too caught up in her memories to worry about how much she was revealing. It was the truth, and suddenly she had a burning impulse to unburden herself of it. 'I felt so connected to you and I needed that.'

She pressed a hand to her stomach, remembering what it had been like to be pregnant. 'Finding out I was pregnant was a lifeline when I needed it most. A baby bound me to the outside world, to you and to Lewis. A baby was someone to be strong for.'

He moved closer, pressing his forehead to hers. 'You are so strong, Annabelle. The strongest person I've ever known.'

She lifted her shoulders. 'I've been what I had to be.'

His breath whispered against her cheek. 'Seeing the way my mother suffered because of my dad, I can't believe how *you've* suffered.'

'It's not the same.'

'Really? Because I have the strangest sense that history's been repeating itself.'

'Your dad was indifferent to your mum's situation. You didn't know about mine.'

There was silence in the room, just the sound of his breathing and hers mingling, mixing, faster than breathing should have been given that they were sitting down.

'I would have done this sooner if I had.'

She couldn't say why, but his words didn't relax her. If anything, it was a reminder that their whole situation came down to his sense of duty and obligation, rather than anything to do with him wanting to be with her by choice.

'Have you really not had the opportunity to meet anyone since me?'

'I haven't had the inclination,' she murmured huskily. Then, thinking it sounded as though she'd been pining for him, she quickly added, 'I had to be a mum and dad for Max. I wanted him to know that I was always there for him.' She bit down on her lip. 'Between Max and work, I've had my hands full.'

More silence, heavier this time, and with every second that passed Annie felt her awareness of Dimitrios increasing until her blood felt as though it had turned to lava in her veins.

'And you?' she whispered in an attempt to hold on to sanity, to remember who they were and what this marriage was really about. 'I suppose life went on as usual for you.'

A frown briefly marred his handsome face. 'Largely, yes.' There was an uneasiness in admitting that.

Her smile showed a hint of sadness. 'Relax. It was one night. It's not like I expected you to stay celibate afterwards.' She laughed to put him at ease but it sounded brittle, even to her own ears.

'The thing is, I was so full of regrets.'

She flinched a little, but didn't move away.

'Sleeping with you was a betrayal of my closest friend. I'd promised Lewis I'd look out for you and instead I'd done the exact opposite. I was harsher to you than I needed to be, simply because I had to make sure you didn't continue to harbour any feelings for me. At the time, I was sure that I was doing the right thing.' His smile was tight. 'I wanted to forget you.'

Realisation dawned. 'So you did what you could to make that happen? Sleeping with other women to expunge me from your memory?'

His eyes widened. 'Not consciously. And not so cynically. But, yes, Annabelle. I hoped I would simply forget you as time went on.'

She knew that he hadn't, though. He'd already said as much.

His voice was a husky growl. 'I wish I could tell you something different.'

She shook her head. 'Why?'

'Because you deserve that.'

Her stomach squeezed. 'You never made me any promises, Dimitrios.'

'Didn't I?' His smile was ghost-like. He stood, and the distance he put between them was like a yawning barrier she ached to cross. 'Perhaps you're right. But I've made you promises now, Annabelle. I won't hurt you like that again. I will never let our chemistry dictate what happens between us—if we sleep together, it will be because you decide it's right, not because our bodies can't control themselves. And I will do whatever I can to make you happy here in this marriage. Okay?'

CHAPTER NINE

SHE COULDN'T STOP thinking about him. It was as if a switch had been flicked, in the week since they'd spoken in the lounge she preferred, with the tropical rain lashing against the windows. She caught his eyes often and, every time that happened, heat bloomed in her cheeks. She watched him when she should have been doing other things. She imagined him undressed—pictured his abdominals, his tanned skin, his broad shoulders. She found herself daydreaming about him and, when it came to actually sleeping in the same bed as him yet not touching, Annie was fighting a losing battle.

Each night, Annie felt as though she were burning alive, lying only a few feet away from him on their separate sides of the bed. She was so careful not to move, not to stir, not to reach out and drag her nails down his back, cup his buttocks. Temptation was driving her crazy.

It wasn't just sensual heat, though. It was so much more.

Dimitrios was an amazing father. Watching him bond with Max convinced her, every day, that she'd made the right decision. Seeing them together made her feel a happiness she'd never known. It wasn't even as if they were slowly building a relationship. Something had clicked inside Max the moment he'd met Dimitrios. It was easy and natural, as though they'd been together from birth. The night before, she'd watched Max and Dimitrios play cards for hours, while she'd pretended to read a book. But her concentration had been shot, so in the end she'd given up and simply enjoyed the sight of her son playing his favourite game—and winning by no small margin.

Yet every time Dimitrios had lifted his gaze and looked at Annie, her heart had skipped a beat, her stomach had tied itself in knots and she'd felt a surge of need that had had nothing to do with Dimitrios's paternal abilities and everything to do with him and her.

'Good morning.' She startled, shifting in the bed a little, wondering how he'd known she was awake. Usually one of them got up before the other, avoiding the intimacy of speaking while they were lying down side by side. Silly, really, given that they'd created a child together.

She rolled over, wondering why she didn't feel more self-conscious about her natural state— no make-up, hair a mess, wearing only a pair of pyjamas she'd had for years. Annie's lips lifted into a small smile. 'Good morning.'

'Are you busy today?'

Annie shook her head. She'd kept on a few clients, but the workload was much lighter than before, and she'd been able to finish up for Christmas.

'Why do you ask?'

'Francesca is taking Max to that soccer workshop.' He reminded her that the lovely nanny he'd hired had scheduled some holiday activities for Max—many of them with pupils from the school he'd be attending—and he was already starting to make friends. How quickly it was all falling into place!

'That's right. He was so excited about that.'

'Yes.' Dimitrios's smile showed pride, but the way his eyes were roaming over her face made it hard to concentrate on anything except the fact there was only about eight inches between them—and how badly she wanted to close them.

'So,' he drawled, 'I was thinking it would be a good opportunity.'

'For what?' she enquired on a snagged breath.

'To go Christmas shopping.'

It was such a perfect suggestion, she should have been excited, but there was a part of Annie that was screaming in complaint. What had she hoped he'd say—that they stay home and make love all day?

He was waiting for *her* to suggest that. He'd made it obvious it would only happen if and when she said she was ready. And what if she could never screw up the courage?

The idea of that made breathing difficult. What was she waiting for? Why wasn't she telling him how much she wanted him?

'You mentioned you'd been saving up for Max,' he murmured, reaching out and putting a hand on hers. It was a simple touch but it sent a jolt running through her and she visibly startled, her eyes flying wide open. 'You don't need to worry about money. I want you to get him whatever you want. And I want to come—to help choose some gifts for him.'

Her fingers were tingling beneath his. 'That's very…thoughtful. But surely you're too busy?'

His expression shifted a little. 'If you'd prefer to do it alone, I understand.'

'No.' She shook her head, rushing to correct his misunderstanding. 'I didn't mean that.'

'It's fine,' he said gently. 'It's been just you and Max for a long time. I didn't mean to rush you. We can leave things as they have been—you do the shopping. I'll help next year.'

Next year. It was such a promise of permanence and longevity! It was hard to get her head around that. Besides, he was right: this would take time. He was being so reasonable and understanding, so accommodating of her needs.

'It's not that. I'd like you to come. I honestly meant what I said—that I presumed you'd be too busy.' A frown crossed her face. 'I don't want you feeling that you have to rearrange your life for us.'

A pause followed, then he leaned closer. 'I don't feel that I have to. I want to.'

Lightness spread through her; a smile followed. 'Then let's do it.'

* * *

At some point since Sydney, he'd stopped thinking of her as Lewis's sister. He'd stopped thinking of her as a mistake from his past and started seeing her as she was. And Annabelle Papandreo was completely captivating. His eyes followed as she browsed the toy aisle, carefully lifting boxes from the shelf, looking at them for several moments, reading the back, then more often than not replacing them in their spot. He was pushing a trolley that remained empty. If it had been up to him, it would be half-full by now. At least.

'What exactly is the selection criteria?'

She turned to face him, her smile like sunshine. His chest compressed in response. 'It's complicated.'

'Hit me with it.'

She grinned. 'Really, I'm just looking for something he'll love.'

Dimitrios bent down and picked up the box she'd most recently discarded. 'And you don't think he'd love this?'

'Oh, he undoubtedly would.'

'So why not get it?'

'Because it's not perfect.'

'And you want to get him just one perfect gift?'

She tilted her head to the side. 'I usually get him a few things. The things he's asked for and something I choose—a book, perhaps some tennis balls.' She shrugged. 'We used to go down to the park on weekends and play tennis, you know. He's actually very good.'

Dimitrios felt pride swell in his breast. Their son was good at many things. Cards, conversation, reading and, yes, he believed sports too.

'And even though you could buy this store ten times over and not see a dent in your bank account?' he prompted.

Her eyes grew round. 'I'd never do that.'

He smiled, moving closer, an urge to kiss her almost overtaking him. 'I know.'

'I guess I don't want him to feel like his life has changed too much.'

Dimitrios bit back a laugh; Annabelle didn't. The sound was self-mocking. 'I know how ridiculous that sounds. I mean, look where we're living. I had to ask the housekeeper to stop making his bed the other day because that's a job Max has always done for himself.' Her smile was rueful. 'I just don't want him to get used to all this. To think it's normal.'

That sent a jolt of warning through Dimitrios.

'What's wrong with getting used to it?' Only, she didn't need to voice the fear she had. It was obvious to him. He moved closer then, pressing his finger beneath her chin, lifting her face to his. 'We're married now, Annabelle. None of this is going away.'

Her eyes were suddenly suspiciously moist. His chest felt as if a bag of cement were pressing down on it.

'I know you say that, but...'

A tear formed on her lashes, making them clump together. He was conscious of holding his breath as she searched for the right words. When she spoke, her voice was barely a whisper. 'Everyone's always gone away.'

Her eyes didn't meet his and he was glad. He wasn't sure what his expression would show, but he felt as though she'd reached into his chest and hollowed him out.

She was right.

Lewis had died. And then her parents had moved to Perth. Then he'd got her pregnant and disappeared out of her life into a world that, to a teenaged Annabelle, must have seemed like a million miles away.

She'd been alone for ever, fighting her own

corner, looking after her son all by herself. No wonder she felt as if all this might be transient.

'This is for keeps.'

Her smile was brief. Dismissive. He shook his head and moved closer. 'I don't make promises I don't mean.'

Her eyes lifted to his and he felt a thousand and one things slamming into him. Mostly, he wanted to make her smile again, to make her truly happy. She was the mother of his child, so that was only natural. How could Max thrive if he didn't have a happy mum?

'Think about it, Annabelle. Why would I have suggested we get married if it wasn't a permanent arrangement?'

She nodded awkwardly. 'I know. You could have taken Max away from me without breaking a sweat.' Her eyes were troubled at the prospect of that. 'I'm grateful you didn't.'

'I don't want your gratitude.'

Her eyes held the hint of a challenge. 'What do you want, then?'

Great question. The answer was harder to voice than it should have been. 'I want to take it one day at a time, but I know I want you and Max here with me. Or wherever I am. It just feels… right.'

It was how they'd described the night they'd spent together. It was a word that kept coming up when they spoke. 'Right'. It was right that they'd got married. Right that they'd come to Singapore.

She pulled away from him, nodding vaguely, a smile on her lips that didn't reach her eyes. 'Yes, okay.' She reached out and grabbed a box, putting it in the trolley. 'Maybe this one.'

She hadn't even looked at the gift to see what it was.

Frustration zipped inside Dimitrios. He'd disappointed her. He'd given the wrong answer. What had she expected him to say? What had she wanted?

He ground his teeth together, following just a little behind her, his eyes scanning the rows of gifts.

Half an hour later, Annabelle had chosen a few more, with more care, each assessed for several minutes until, with a small nod, she'd decided they were suitable and had slipped them into the trolley. It was hardly what Dimitrios would describe as a 'haul'. A remote-controlled car, a motorised train for Max's train set and a soccer shirt.

They'd agreed they didn't want to spoil him, yet as Dimitrios's first Christmas with Max he found it hard not to throw every damned toy into the trolley. The idea of Max waking up to see the tree littered with presents with his name on them made Dimitrios feel all warm inside.

But their first instincts had been right. He was a great kid. Kind, generous, loving, happy. There was no need to fill his world with material things. Besides, he was living in a mansion with an army of staff at his disposal, his every whim catered for. Normal life was in his rearview mirror, and Dimitrios knew for himself how unsettling that change was to make.

'You know,' he said as they left the department store and entered the opulent walkway of the mall, decorated for Christmas almost as thoroughly as his home. 'I've been thinking about your law degree.'

'I didn't get a law degree,' she reminded him.

'You couldn't, because of Max. But he's at school now, and you don't need to work—or not as many hours as you have been. You could study, if you wanted.'

Her surprise was evident, as though it hadn't even occurred to her. 'I could, couldn't I?'

Something lifted inside him, his mood shifting. It was just what she needed to underscore the permanence of this. A life outside him and Max—a life that would fulfil her and make her happy. 'Lewis always said you were the smartest person he'd ever met.'

Her eyes flashed to his, showing happiness. 'Did he?'

'Yeah. Present company included.'

She was smiling properly now, the look on her face making him feel a thousand kilograms lighter.

'I'd want to see Max settled into school properly first,' she was murmuring. 'But after the first term, once I knew he was making friends and doing okay, then I wouldn't feel so bad about doing something for me.'

'And it doesn't have to be law. You could study whatever you want.'

She laughed. 'You don't have to sell me on it, Dimitrios. I get it. It's a good idea.' Her voice was warm and soft. She slowed down a little, and emotion sparked in her eyes once more. 'Thank you.'

'You don't have to thank me.'

She lifted her shoulders. 'It wouldn't have occurred to me. And I love the idea.'

'Great. I'll have one of my assistants look into it.'

She shook her head reproachfully, a smile making her eyes sparkle. 'I can look into it myself.'

Relief flooded him. 'Keep me posted?'

'Can I open them yet?'

'Almost.' Dimitrios grinned, his hands covering Annabelle's eyes, his body guiding her carefully across the marina.

'I can smell the ocean salt.'

'Very perceptive.'

'You're not going to throw me to the sharks, are you?'

'Not yet.'

She laughed. 'I'm serious, Dimitrios. Where are we?'

'Has anyone ever told you that you're bad at surprises?'

'I've had enough surprises to last a lifetime,' she said in a droll tone that made him grin. He'd been smiling a *lot* today, after the heavy emotion of that morning, when she'd confessed her fear that he'd go away just like everyone else had. They'd strolled the mall, window-shopped and Annabelle had shown utter shock at the price of several things. He loved how down to earth she was and wondered if that would change, given her net worth now. Lunch had been at one of his favourite restaurants, and then they'd gone to a gallery, where Annabelle had shown an impressive knowledge of modern artists.

The idea to come here had been spur of the moment. Deep down, Dimitrios admitted to himself that he hadn't been ready for their outing to come to an end. It was a good opportunity to get to know her better, he told himself.

'Okay, almost time.'

At the premier yacht club of Singapore, his boat stood several feet longer and taller than any other. He brought her to a stop at its stern, then slowly eased his hands away from her eyes, letting them drop to her shoulders and mould to her warm skin.

'Can I open my eyes now?'

He looked down at her and something jerked hard inside him, a feeling he couldn't place, a sense of importance and need that he had no idea how to rationalise.

'Yeah, open your eyes.' He cleared his throat, moving his hands and stepping to her side so he could see her reaction.

A divot formed between her brows as she scanned the boats before giving his more attention.

'The Patricia?' she asked with a raised brow.

'My mother.'

'Seriously?' Her smile was gently teasing. He nudged her with his shoulder in response.

'What? Not cool enough for you?'

'It's…' She sobered, shaking her head.

Frustration hit him. He didn't want her to close herself off from him. 'It's what?'

'Sweet.' But her tone was reserved; clipped.

He suppressed his impatience. 'Want to go on board?'

She looked at him for several seconds and he felt as though the world had stopped spinning. He waited, wondering when he'd become someone who sat back and waited rather than just calling all the shots. Wasn't he the kind of man who ordinarily would have said, 'Let's go on the yacht?' Nonetheless, he found himself standing there silently, watchful but not speaking, all his attention focussed on Annabelle.

She turned back to the yacht, her expression impossible to interpret. 'Just for a minute.'

His response was to reach down and take her hand, lacing their fingers together as he guided her to the swim platform.

The wind in Annie's hair made her feel as if she could do anything. She gripped the railing, looking back at Singapore with a sense of lightness and happiness that, contradictorily, made her anxious. She was getting too relaxed, enjoying herself too much. She had to remember that this was all pretend. Even when he was being so ridiculously attentive and sweet, and making her feel as though she was the centre of his universe, it wasn't about Annie so much as Max. All of this was for Max.

Dimitrios wanted them to be happy here, and he knew a big part of that was making Annie happy, so he was being accommodating. It wasn't about her. He was doing what he had to do to protect his son.

The lightness disappeared a little and she felt glad. Better to be aware of her situation at all times than to simply relax and enjoy.

'Do you like it?'

She hadn't realised Dimitrios had joined her; she'd been lost in her own thoughts. She startled a little, turning to face him, then wishing she hadn't. He'd changed into a pair of swimming trunks, a turquoise that made his tan glow like gold, and she found it almost impossible not to let her eyes drop to the expanse of his toned chest. Dark hair arrowed towards his shorts and in the periphery of her vision she followed it then felt heat bloom in her cheeks.

'Do I like…what?' Her voice sounded so thick and hoarse. She cleared her throat but knew it wouldn't help.

'The yacht.'

'Oh.' She nodded. 'Yes.'

His grin showed white teeth. She jerked her head away, but it didn't help. His image was seared into her eyeballs. His proximity made her pulse go haywire.

'Are you going swimming?' The question sounded so prim! She closed her eyes for a moment, wishing she could be effortlessly cool and unimpressed.

'If you'll join me.'

She glanced down at the dark ocean. It was a warm day but the idea of jumping off the back of the boat didn't appeal to her. He lightly pressed a finger to her elbow then ran it down her forearm, teasing her flesh before taking hold of her wrist and lifting it, pointing towards the top of the yacht.

'Up there.'

Closer inspection showed that the top of the yacht had deck chairs, and she could only surmise a pool at its centre.

'You don't think we should be getting back?' They'd been on board for half an hour. 'Just to see the city from a distance.'

'Max is fine. Francesca's with him.'

Dimitrios was right; Annie knew that. Her desire to return to the safety and space of his house had nothing to do with Max and everything to do with the fact she was finding it almost impossible not to obey her body's increasingly demanding needs.

'I don't have any bathers.'

'There are plenty in the bedroom. Come. I'll show you.' He caught her hand once more, pulling on it gently so she collided with his naked chest. Her breath burst from her lips. She stared up at him, her pulse hammering hard, his eyes boring down into hers speculatively.

'Or you could swim without.' The words were said low and deep, a husky invitation that had her knees quivering.

She swallowed a groan, but found she couldn't deny how tempted she was. Apparently, he took her silence as a rebuke, because he squeezed her hand. 'Relax, Annabelle. It was a joke.'

Disappointment seared her. She wanted to tell him she was fine with going naked, that it was no big deal to strip out of her clothes and let him see her as she was, but something held her back.

'How come you call me Annabelle?' She blurted out the question instead, causing him to frown.

'It's your name, right?'

'I mean, when everyone else calls me Annie.'

He lifted one shoulder. 'Maybe I don't like to be the same as everyone else.'

Fat chance, she thought with a smile. Dimitrios Papandreo could *never* be like anyone else on earth, ever.

He began to walk across the deck and into a window-filled corridor, and she fell into step beside him. A bedroom came off it to one side, but not like any bedroom she might have expected to see, had she put any thought into such matters. No, this room was spacious and decorated more like a bedroom in a five-star hotel than on a boat. An enormous king-size bed sat at its centre, a huge mirror framed in pale timber hung behind it, and there was cream-coloured carpet underfoot. The furniture was Scandinavian in style, and a huge wardrobe boasted a selection of clothes—male and female. A wisp of jealousy breathed through her, unmistakable and sharp. Who were the clothes for? Who'd worn them?

'I had a selection sent here after your shopping trip in Sydney,' he said, as though he could read her thoughts. She moved closer and saw that, as with the wardrobe selection then, these had their tags still attached.

It was so thoughtful and unexpected, though it shouldn't have been. If she knew anything about Dimitrios, it was that he was prepared for anything.

'I like to have stuff at each of my places,' he explained. 'Saves having to pack much when I travel.'

She reached for one of the dresses, feeling the silk fabric beneath her fingertips, her lips twisting in a smile that was bittersweet. 'Exactly how many homes do you have?'

'Singapore is my home,' he said, surprising her by coming to stand right behind her. 'But I have properties around the world, mainly in the places we do the most business—London, Madrid, Tokyo, New York, Paris, Dubai, Sydney.'

Her head was spinning.

'Did you come back to Sydney often after—' She forced herself to finish the question, though she wasn't sure where it had come from. 'After that night?'

His eyes flashed at hers, hesitation obvious in their dark depths. 'Not often.'

'But you did come back?'

His nostrils flared as he exhaled, evidently choosing his words wisely. 'We have business there. It's where my mum lives. Yes, I came back.'

Her stomach looped. The idea that he'd been in the same city as Max and not known about him made everything feel so much worse. At that moment, the boat began to move, as though it had come across the wake of another craft, just little shifts in the current that caused it to rock—and to rock enough that Annie lost her footing ever so slightly.

Dimitrios's response was instant, snaking a

hand out to catch her elbow, holding her steady. It was the lightest touch, and for an obvious purpose, but it set her pulse skittering wildly. All she was conscious of was his nearness and strength, the warmth of his touch, his overtly masculine bearing, the woody citrus fragrance he wore. And suddenly she was riding a different wave, this one not gentle or slow, but dragging her higher and higher in an inescapable current. Her eyes lifted to his and she felt something lock into place—the culmination of everything she'd been feeling and wanting all day and the certainty that, though she might wonder at her decision, she knew it was the only decision she could make.

Her hands lifted to his bare chest, her fingers splaying wide over his pectoral muscles. She dropped her gaze to them, staring at her fingertips, her mouth dryer than the desert.

'The bathing costumes are in the drawer.' It was gruff. She noticed he didn't take a step backward, though. If anything, he moved slightly closer, so his hips brushed hers, sending a riot of awareness tumbling through her body.

She was scared but she was also bold—she knew what she wanted—and that certainty meant she was going to see this through, come what may. Her eyes held his, a challenge in their depths as her fingers found the hem of her shirt. She lifted it slowly, not looking away from his face, so she recognised the moment his expression shifted and his lips parted on a hiss of breath, his features being pulled tight.

'Help me get changed?' she murmured as she pushed the shirt over her head and dropped it to the floor.

His eyes fell to her lace-clad breasts, his concentration so fierce she could feel heat radiating from him to her.

'Annabelle...' It was a plea. A desperate, aching plea. 'You don't know what you're saying.'

She reached behind her back, finding the bra clasp and undoing it. 'I beg your pardon, but yes, I do.'

She undid the bra, dropping it from the edge of her fingertips so that her breasts spilled out, her nipples taut, begging for his attention.

He swore softly, but everything was magnified; she heard it and it ricocheted through her soul like an earthquake.

'Make love to me, Dimitrios. I don't want to wait any longer.'

CHAPTER TEN

DISBELIEF ETCHED LINES about his mouth but then he shook his head, as though waking from a dream, and a second later crushed his lips to hers, a kiss designed to taste, torment, dominate and give.

She surrendered to it completely, but only for a second, then desperate hunger—starvation—was taking over, ripping her body apart piece by piece, and she was certain he was the only way she could be built back together again.

Her arms wrapped around his neck, pulling her higher up his body and, understanding her silent plea, he lifted her against him, wrapping her legs around his waist as he moved towards the bed, his hands so strong and commanding, his body so warm and masculine. She was melting against him, her insides turning to mush, heat slicking her feminine core, nipples aching for his touch. She arched her back, his name a curse and a spell on her lips, an incantation she offered again and again, her voice barely recognisable.

He kissed through her words, swallowing them whole, his hands working the button at her waist and pushing her trousers down, his fingers lingering tantalisingly on the curves of her calves before reaching her ankles, caressing the flesh there, then the soles of her feet. She whimpered at the lightness of his touch, wanting more, simultaneously relishing everything about this— the desire to stretch it out, to make every second last a lifetime. She wanted to hold on to this.

I'm not going anywhere.

Her heart trilled in her chest. She reached for his shoulders, her nails scoring the flesh there, her back tilting. His lips on her knee surprised her; she startled in response to the unexpected touch and his hands reached for her hips, holding her steady as his mouth made its way slowly, oh, so slowly higher, his tongue teasing the flesh of her inner thigh inch by inch, her breath fast and loud as he went higher still. One hand left her hip, pushing her legs apart, and it didn't occur to her not to comply. She lifted her feet on to the edge of the bed and his mouth came between her legs, his tongue so light she could barely feel it at first, so light it left her desperate—utterly, incandescently desperate—for more.

Still, she wasn't prepared for the experience that was coming—his mouth closing over her most sensitive cluster of nerves and kissing her there until she almost passed out from pleasure. Her fingernails pushed into his shoulders and somewhere in the very, very distant recesses of her mind still capable of thought, she worried she might draw blood.

And yet she couldn't stop.

She couldn't change anything about what they were doing; this was a juggernaut and they were both on board it, just as they'd been that night seven years earlier.

'You're so wet,' he growled, the words so deep they reached inside her and sent tremors of pleasure radiating through her body. His fingers moved to echo his mouth's movements, slipping inside her and finding her raging pulse, until she tipped over the edge of sanity and existence and became a pile of nerves. She cried out as pleasure swallowed her. His name at first, and then just moans, over and over, her body racked with shakes of euphoria.

He didn't give her time to recover. A second later he was kissing his way up her body, his hands still pleasuring her womanhood, his mouth taking a nipple hostage, pressing it hard against his lips, then lightly, so the contrast was too much to bear. She cried out, and he brushed his hair-roughened chin across her chest to the other breast, subjecting that nipple to the same exquisite pleasure-pain.

'Stay here,' he groaned as he reached her mouth, his lips tantalisingly close to hers. 'Don't move.' His eyes bored into hers, as though he was afraid she was going to change her mind. Not a chance in hell.

'Where are you going?'

'To get protection.' A frown creased his perfectly symmetrical brow. 'Unless you want to start trying for another child right away?'

Nothing could dampen the pleasure she was feeling, but his words pulled her some of the way back to sanity. Another child? Another chance to experience motherhood, without the stress she'd known constantly since Max's birth? But, no. That wasn't something you just went into lightly. She needed to think about it, make sure it was the right decision. She shook her head, smiling to hide how tumultuously affected she was by that idea. 'I'm not ready.'

A firm nod from him and then he was gone, walking across the room before disappearing through the door and reappearing less than a minute later, a string of metallic squares dangling from his fingertips, his body now completely naked. His grin showed he wasn't at all affected by her decision about the casually suggested next child, but she barely registered his facial expression. Her entire attention was taken by his physique—his strength, his perfectly honed body, his lithe grace, his easy athleticism, and the impossible-to-miss state of arousal. Her eyes clung to his erection, a hint of panic spearing through her at the idea of *that* fitting inside her.

'God, you're beautiful.' Pleasure spread through her at his compliment. No, not just at the compliment, but the way it sounded—as though it had been wrenched from the heart of his soul, as though he couldn't not say it because he felt it with every fibre of his being. It was though he was marvelling at her, worshipping her, even.

'You've changed since that night. These are

bigger.' He reached for her breasts, cupping them in his hands, his fingers brushing over her nipples.

They were. After Max, her breasts had never gone back to their previous size, though they were still modest.

'You're beautiful,' he said again, shaking his head with a rueful grin before bringing his mouth to hers, kissing her until she was breathless and starlight danced behind her eyelids. She groaned, lifting her legs around his waist, holding him tight.

'I was just thinking the same thing about you.'

She felt his smile against her shoulder and then he was pushing up, running his hand over the side of her face, his eyes searching hers, as though he wanted to say something to her but couldn't find the words. She held her breath anyway, her heart beating overtime, and in her mind she knew what she wanted to hear.

Her eyes flew wide but there was no time to process the foolishness of what she was hoping for—the idea that Dimitrios might love her. If she'd had time to consider it, she might have realised how foolish it was to cement their arrangement with this next step, but he was already parting her legs and pushing his arousal against her womanhood, and animal instincts took over, shoving worry, thought and perception clear from her mind.

She tilted her hips, welcoming him even as he pushed deeper, slowly at first, so she dug her nails into his side and groaned, 'Please, now,' until he drove himself the rest of the way, deep, hard and fast, just as she longed for. His length filled her so she needed a second to adjust to the sensation of his possession, but only a second, and then he was moving again, each thrust of his length exactly what she needed, so she found herself tipping closer to the edge of pleasure. Her fingers sunk into the mattress, her hands curling round the soft sheets, ripping them loose from the bed as she surrendered to the moment, lost on a wave of perfection and euphoria.

She rode that intense wave of pleasure until it crashed around her, spreading heat through her entire body, her head thrashing from side to side, her moans filling the luxurious bedroom, the waves rocking the boat nothing to the waves that were rocking her soul.

As with her last orgasm, he waited only a moment for her breath to slow and then he was moving again, expertly shifting her body a little so she was on her side. Each movement he made reached different parts of her, sending new shockwaves of awareness tearing through her; his hands on her breasts was the last straw, each touch of her nipples seeming to light a fire inside her that there could be no hope of extinguishing.

Their faces were an inch apart, his eyes on hers the whole time, watching her, reading her, trying to understand her, and the intensity of his gaze added a whole new level of intimacy to the experience. A tear rolled down her cheek; she was powerless to stop it. He leaned forward and kissed it, then moved his mouth to hers so she tasted saltiness and passion. This kiss was soft, gentle, stirring something deep in her belly, even as heat and passion coursed through her veins.

He growled low in his throat, moved harder and faster and this time, when pleasure wrenched her from Earth and spirited her far into the heavens, he released himself with one deep, passionate thrust, spilling his seed from his body, her name on his lips filling the room, mingling with her fervent cries, a harmony of intense pleasure and need.

Afterwards, there was not silence, so much as

music. The rhythm of their breathing, the humming she made as she tried to process the extent of their pleasure, the rocking of the boat like a dance into which they were being drawn.

Tension had been dogging Annie for a long time. Seven years? It was as though it had been building ever since that night and now it had finally broken; like the bursting of a dam, something had been loosened and Annie felt…free. She smiled. It was like a weight being lifted from her chest. She'd come home.

Home.

She lifted a hand to his chest, her fingertips pressing against his sternum, so she could feel the solid beating of his heart. She closed her eyes, a smile tingling her lips as she sighed.

Exhaustion was chasing pleasure. She felt as though she could sleep for a week.

But there was a normal life to get back to.

Max.

Her eyes flew open. Dimitrios was watching her, so her heart rate kicked up a notch, renewed desire firing in the pit of her stomach. And even as his arousal was filling her, she felt as though she wanted him all over again.

She ran her fingers sideways, finding his nipple and brushing it slowly. To her surprise, he made a growling noise, as though the same pleasure that had filled her at his touch was now moving through him.

She wanted to explore this, to learn how to pleasure him. No, she wanted to learn how to drive him crazy, how to make him feel a thousand and one things, including the complete loss of control she'd experienced. For years Annie had lain dormant, the sexuality he'd stirred completely disregarded in her day-to-day existence, but now it was bursting to life inside her, refusing to be contained. She had a hunger; she had no idea if she could ever control it.

But Max…

'I hate to say this, but we really should think about going back.'

His fingertip traced a line from her chin to her shoulder, then across her clavicle to the indent at the base of her throat. It was such a light touch, but his familiarity and possessive confidence was a whole new level of sensuality.

'Why?' he murmured.

A smile shifted across her lips.

'Because we have a son.'

We have a son. It was a statement of fact but

the 'we' came so naturally to her lips, and the sharing of Max. They had a son together. Max would always bind them.

I'm not going anywhere.

Euphoria spread through her body, reaching her fingers and toes and everything in between.

'He's with Francesca.'

'But the soccer day will be over by now.'

'So she'll give him dinner and put him to bed.'

Annie frowned. She'd never missed a single night of tucking Max in. Not once. But he wasn't a clingy child, and he adored Francesca.

For six years she'd put him first, prioritising his needs above her own. It hadn't been hard— she was a mother and that instinct had come naturally and with a strength she dared not defy. But for the first time in a long time, lying here with Dimitrios, the waves lapping gently at the side of the boat, she felt a pull to be selfish. To put herself first, just this once.

'You think he'll be okay?' she wondered, seeking reassurance even when she knew he'd be fine.

Dimitrios's smile had the power of a thousand suns. 'I wouldn't suggest it if not.'

Annie relaxed, letting her body go limp and

her eyes close, moving closer to Dimitrios so her head was buried in the crook formed by his arm and his chest. 'We'll call him later, though?' she said softly.

'Yes. We can call him later.'

Dimitrios took a moment to let the feeling pass. Panic gripped him, vice-like and hard. Annabelle snuggled against him and he felt as though he suddenly couldn't breathe, as though he was trapped in a place he'd never wanted to be. Married. Intimacy. This was all so new to him.

For many years, he'd promised himself this was a situation in which he'd never find himself. He'd slept with women—of course—but he'd never stayed the night. Even before Annabelle that had never been his inclination but, after their disastrous night, and realising how badly he'd hurt her, he'd taken an incredible degree of care not to inadvertently lead a woman on. He drew clear lines between sex and anything more, making sure he was absolutely open about what he could offer, what he wanted.

But Annabelle wasn't just another woman, she was his wife, and besides, despite his usual proclivities, there was nowhere else he wanted to be than here, like this, with her. Her head against his chest had grown heavy, her breathing steady. She was asleep. He shifted a little, checking the time on his wristwatch, a slow smile spreading over his face. They had all night—and he was going to make the most of it.

'And this is Annie.'

Lewis reached across, tussling his little sister's blonde hair, earning an eye-roll from her. But, as her vibrant blue eyes shifted to Dimitrios and Zach, bright pink colour infused her cheeks and her full lips parted on a husky breath.

'Hey, good to meet you.'

Zach extended a hand, grinning as she took it and smiled in response. Dimitrios, though, stood stock-still. She was nothing like Lewis, who was dark in complexion and colouring, though their eyes had a similar shape. And there was something in the quizzical force of her expression, intelligent eyes that he somehow just knew would miss very little.

'We're heading away for the weekend,' Lewis said. 'Are Mum and Dad home?'

Annie's eyes lingered on Dimitrios before shifting to look at Lewis. 'Dad is—upstairs.'

'And Mum?'

Annie shrugged, but there was tension in those shoulders, a look in her eyes that spoke of pain.

Dimitrios wanted to know everything about that—why was she troubled?

Lewis didn't speak of his parents often. But he talked about his sister constantly. Dimitrios wasn't sure why, but he'd pictured Annie as younger than she was—perhaps that was just Lewis's big brotherly, protective vibe, making it seem as if he had a kid sister rather than someone on the brink of womanhood.

Womanhood? Christ. She was a teenager. Fifteen? But, yes, she was on the cusp—and why the hell was he noticing the fullness of her curves, the sweetness of her smile? He needed to get a grip.

'We should get going, Lewis.'

'Right.' Lewis put an arm around Annie's shoulders, drawing her close. 'Annie, entertain these guys while I go pack. Won't be long.'

Dimitrios watched as Annie and Zach fell into an easy rhythm, chatting about anything, from the local area to her schoolwork, to the law degree she was already set on pursuing.

'I do really well in legal studies,' she said with a small smile.

Dimitrios noticed that she barely looked in his direction. But he looked at her. He found it almost impossible not to.

'Law is so dry, though, so boring,' Zach was teasing, a grin on his face.

'I like boring.'

She laughed, a sound like a bell ringing. Then her eyes dipped furtively towards him and her smile dropped, a frown taking its place before she looked away again quickly—but not before he could see the pink in her cheeks again.

'Would you like a drink?' she asked Zach, but she gestured towards Dimitrios too, encompassing him in the invitation.

'Nah, we've got water bottles in the car.'

'I'll have a coffee,' Dimitrios was surprised to hear himself say.

Hadn't he been telling Lewis to hurry up only a minute earlier? So why prolong their time in this house?

'O-okay...' She stuttered a little, dipping her head forward so a curtain of blonde covered her face. 'How do you take it?'

'Black, strong.'

She lifted her eyes to his then and something fizzed between them—something that made sense of what he'd been feeling.

She had a crush on him!

That was why he was watching her like a hawk, trying to understand her behaviour towards him. She was young, inexperienced and her hormone-driven mind had cast him as some kind of romantic hero. Wasn't that what teenage girls did?

He smiled to soften her nervousness, but it seemed to have the opposite effect.

'I won't be long.'

He startled, shifting in the bed, casting another glance at his gold wristwatch. Only ten minutes had elapsed but he'd dozed off, the past beckoning him, dragging him towards recollections he hadn't thought of in years. The first time he'd met Annabelle she had made an impression on him. Even then there'd been something about her that had got under his skin—and it wasn't simply that she'd had a crush on him. No, he'd found her every gesture intriguing, and he'd wanted to sit there and decode her, to make sense of her. Whenever Lewis had spoken of her after that, he'd listened with extra attentiveness. Particularly when she'd started dating some boy from a neighbouring school two years older than her. Lewis hadn't really liked the guy. 'But it's her life,' he'd said with a shrug. 'And she clearly thinks he's great.'

That had been the end of it. Or so Dimitrios had told himself. Then why had he gone to Annabelle the night after the funeral? It had been more than just checking up on her. It had been way more than his promise to Lewis. He'd felt compelled to see her, as though she was exactly where he needed to be.

He shifted a little in the bed, moving so he could see her, and something lurched inside him.

For whatever reason he'd gone to her, she'd deserved better. He'd had no idea she'd been a virgin; how could he have? She'd had boyfriends by then. Why would he presume a woman of eighteen hadn't had sex when she'd been dating? Would it have changed anything about that night? That was something he couldn't answer with any certainty.

He moved again and this time Annabelle stirred, slowly blinking up at him, the clarity of her eyes jettisoning him into the past at the same time she propelled him into the future, so he was at sixes and sevens with no clear notion of where he was in time or place.

'I fell asleep.' She smiled apologetically, only the slightest hint of the teenager he'd first met lingering in her eyes and on her lips.

'Do you want to sleep some more?' he asked, even as every bone in his body was silently praying she'd say no.

She shook her head, shyness flooding her eyes. 'That's the last thing I want.'

A second later, she'd lifted up and straddled him, her expression showing sensual heat. A second after that and her lips were on his, her flesh pressed to him, so thoughts and memories all burst into flames; there was only Annabelle, there was only this…

CHAPTER ELEVEN

'I DON'T WANT this to happen,' she sobbed, hugging Lewis close, his frail frame in the bed bringing a lump to her throat that she couldn't clear.

'We don't have any say in that.' Even in his weakened condition, he smiled, trying to ease her pain. 'Listen to me, Annie. I'm tired. I don't know how long I'll have, but it can't be long. The drugs make me feel loopy most of the time,' he said, referring to the cocktail of pain medication he'd been prescribed.

'I know.'

She sat on the edge of his bed, stroking his hand. In the space of three months, he'd gone from looking strong and vital to this—pale and barely a skeleton with skin.

'You are my favourite person in the whole world.' He turned over his hand, catching hers. 'You're so smart and so kind and so funny—you are going to live a wonderful life.'

A sob racked her lungs.

'I need you to do something for me.'

She nodded urgently. 'Anything.'

'Live your life for me. Remember how proud I am of you. Remember how much faith I have in you. Remember the stories I've told you about everything you deserve and don't ever settle for anything less. You're brilliant, Annie. You deserve the world.'

The memory had come to her out of nowhere, hovering on the brink of her mind as she woke early the next morning. Their night had been perfect. After the boat, they'd gone to an exclusive club, where Dimitrios had sat close to Annie she had drunk a cocktail and felt as though she were floating in heaven. Neither of them had seemed to want the night to end. They'd come home in the small hours of the morning and they'd made love again in the bed that Annie now thought of as theirs until her body had been weakened by pleasure and she'd been too tired to keep her eyes open.

Everything was perfect.

Except it wasn't. It just *looked* perfect.

The distinction sat in her gut as she dressed

that morning and, despite the corner they'd turned, she felt a sense of panic crowding her.

They'd become intimate but that didn't really mean anything—at least, not in the sense she wanted it to.

Out of nowhere, with the force of a lightning bolt, she remembered the detail of when they'd been making love on the boat and she'd wanted, more than anything, for him to tell her he loved her. How she'd craved those words—words she knew she'd never hear him offer.

Dimitrios went to work and she was glad of that. She needed space to fathom what she wanted next, what their new level of intimacy meant and, more importantly, she needed to work out how to exist in a marriage that included friendship and sex but no love. Weren't the lines getting far more blurred than either of them had intended?

Fortunately, Max was in one of his million-miles-an-hour moods, so it was hard for Annie to focus on anything but him. Even when her mind kept throwing flashbacks at her—reminding her of the pleasure she'd felt the night before, of the man who'd driven her wild—she forced herself to stay in the present. One foot after the other, breathing in and out, until the day was almost at an end.

In the way of children, Max barely seemed to feel the heat of Singapore. He wanted to go out and explore, and Annie agreed, so they asked the driver to take them into the city. They shopped and found a playground, then the driver took them to a food market full of local delicacies. They weren't too adventurous with their selections, but what they did order was delicious, and Annie promised they'd come back another time.

Christmas was everywhere they looked—despite the heat, as in Australia the depictions and decorations were all of a northern hemisphere, wintry Christmas. Trees with white snow painted on their ends, windows that looked snow-covered. Annie bought a packet of gourmet fruit mince pies on autopilot—it was something she'd always loved as a child but had had to do without since Max.

As the evening drew closer, nervous anticipation began to seep into her body. Soon they'd be home and that would mean facing Dimitrios. Annie knew she had to work out what she wanted before then. If she didn't? They'd go to bed together, and again and again, and a pattern would form that would set the tone for the rest of her life. Which was fine, if she could accept what he was offering.

But was it enough?

She looked down at Max and guilt rammed her. How could she even think it wouldn't be? How could she think her feelings mattered at all? This was right for Max, wasn't it?

But her own childhood had been so marred by her parents' unhappy marriage. She knew she had to avoid that too. She wouldn't raise Max in a war zone.

Only, fighting with Dimitrios wasn't inevitable—they could treat each other with respect even if they didn't love one another.

If only Annie could be certain that was the case!

She stopped walking, staring at a glamorous handbag-store as her heart twisted sharply. It *wasn't* the case. They might not love each other but Annie loved Dimitrios. She groaned softly, lifting a hand to her parted lips. She'd loved him as a teenager, but that had been easy to write off as a childish infatuation. This was so different. This was far more adult, far more dangerous, predicated on the way she'd come to know him now, years after they'd conceived Max. He was everything she'd fantasised about back then but so much more, too. He was kind, gentle and thoughtful, considerate and passionate. He was her other half.

'Mummy? What is it?'

She swallowed hard, realisation making her breathing uneven. 'I'm just hot, Maxi.' She reverted to his baby name and he didn't complain.

'We should go home. Or get ice-cream.'

His opportunistic second suggestion brought a vague smile to her face. 'Home for now.'

'Okay.' His voice only sounded a little disappointed. 'It's funny to think of this as home.'

More guilt. What was she actually proposing—that she leave Dimitrios? She couldn't do that to Max, no matter how hard this was for her. But nor could she stay in a sham marriage, could she? She felt as though she were in a small room with daggers on all sides.

'Do you like it here?'

The question was guarded, carefully blanked of any of Annie's own thoughts.

'Oh, yeah. It's great. I love the soccer team, and the school looks awesome. I love the house and the pool and the golf course and my room.'

Annie nodded, difficulties cracking through her mind. 'Good, darling. I'm glad. Now, where's that car…?'

Dimitrios patted the box in his pocket as he strode through the front door, a smile on his face, impatience making his movements swift. His day had been long, far longer than he'd intended. A crisis had blown up with one of his corporate investments—the kind of crisis that would usually necessitate Dimitrios's personal attention, requiring him to jump on the jet and fly straight to Hong Kong to sort it out.

But he didn't. Instead, he did phone conferences and worked over email to resolve the situation, and in the back of his mind was the certainty that he didn't want to leave Annabelle and Max.

His family.

Max was in bed when he returned home. 'I'm late,' he said to Annabelle, shaking his head. 'I couldn't get away sooner.'

Her eyes didn't quite meet his, reminding him of the first time they'd met, that memory still fresh in his mind despite how much had happened—and changed—since then.

'It's fine. He was tired. We walked a lot today.'

He smiled, but also a kernel of jealousy lodged in his chest. He needed to scale back his hours— he should be joining Max as he got to know his new city.

'Where did you go?'

'Everywhere,' she said. 'Are you hungry?'

There was something in her tone that raised a hint of alarm. Instinctively, he wanted to erase that. 'Sure. But first, I have something for you.'

She froze, her body quite still, her eyes wide as they lifted to his. 'Oh?'

He reached for her hand at the same time he removed the jewellery box from his jacket. The world-famous turquoise would communicate to her that something special was inside. He watched as she lifted the lid, her fingers a little unsteady. The ring shone in the light of the hall-way. Large diamonds formed a circlet, and in their centre there was a canary-yellow diamond the size of a fingernail, cut in a perfect circle and set in four shimmering claws. Annabelle stared at it for a long time, as though she'd never seen a ring before.

'It goes on your finger,' he said with a droll smile.

She didn't look at him. 'I know. It's just… Whatever did you buy it for?'

He pulled the ring from the box and took her hand in his, lifting it so he could slip the ring on to her finger.

It was a perfect fit. She flexed her fingers, staring at it, before flicking her eyes in his direction. 'Why are you giving me this?'

He reached for her hand, stroking her fingers. 'Last night felt like a beginning. I wanted to mark the occasion.'

The column of her throat shifted as she swallowed. She looked the opposite of overjoyed. It was as though the ring was some kind of burden. 'Thank you.'

Her reaction wasn't what he'd expected. He spoke carefully, his voice calm, but his every instinct was flaring to life, telling him something was up.

'You don't like it?'

Her white teeth sank into her lower lip. 'It's beautiful,' she contradicted, but so quietly he had to strain to hear. 'It's just…'

'Go on.'

'About last night…'

He braced his skeleton with steel, a sharp rush

of wariness making his body tense all over. 'Yes?'

She sighed. 'I think we need to talk.'

And, just like that, he recognised that he'd been afraid of this all day. It was why he'd stayed local, why he'd moved mountains to be able to come home to her tonight. He'd been worried about her reaction.

Regret. Guilt. Shame. Everything he'd felt after the first time they'd been together came crashing back into him. But this was different—he'd been so careful this time, fighting all his instincts to make sure the time was right for Annabelle, that she was ready.

Except something was bothering her, and that was everything Dimitrios had wanted to avoid. He braced himself for whatever was coming. 'Okay. Let's talk.'

Annie poured two glasses of wine and handed one to him, the ring catching her attention. She stared at it for a few seconds, then moved towards the table nearest the pool. The water was a deep turquoise colour and greenery surrounded them—bougainvillea grew rampant like a purple-flowering wall, giving privacy on one side. The city glistened straight ahead, and geranium and succulents formed a lush garden to their left. She breathed in, the fragrance of this place heaven. Except her nerves were too stretched to enjoy it.

'Well?' He was so formal, an air of caution infusing his words. The man she'd made love to for hours the night before was nowhere to be seen. 'What did you want to talk about?'

She ran her finger over the rim of the glass, forcing herself to rip this plaster off, to be brave even when she knew she could just enjoy the good parts of this life and be done with it.

You have to live your life for me now, Annie.

She sipped her wine, glad of the hit of alcohol. 'I need to know if anything changed for you last night.'

He leaned forward, his fingers linked at the front of the table, his eyes boring into hers. 'Such as?'

A weight dropped inside her. She sipped her wine again, knowing she shouldn't do that—this was definitely a conversation she wanted to be present for, and to have all her brainpower at her disposal. The problem was, if he didn't understand what she was saying then she already had her answer. Nonetheless, she knew she needed to explain.

'You were right about the first time we slept together. It was more than sex for me.'

He stayed ominously silent, and for the first time Annie had a sense of what it would be like to be opposite this man in a combative capacity, of what he must be like in business.

'I think I fell in love with you the first time we met and that never really went away.'

'A girlhood crush,' he dismissed easily, except it *wasn't* easy. She heard the hesitation in his voice, and knew he'd recognised how she felt. How could he have failed to see? She'd worn a huge heart very clearly on her sleeve.

'No, it was more than that. I'd heard Lewis talk about you, so I think even before you and Zach came to our place I was halfway to thinking you were pretty amazing. But something inside me just clicked the day we met.'

'You were fifteen,' he reminded her, a hint of cynicism in his voice.

'Yes. And I tried very hard not to think about you again.'

'Right. You went out with other men,' he pointed out, earning a frown from Annie.

'How do you know who I dated?'

'Lewis mentioned it,' Dimitrios responded tightly.

'Technically, I guess I did date, but really it was just friendships. I didn't ever *feel* anything for anyone. Handsome, intelligent men could chat me up in a bar and I wouldn't have the time of day for them. That's never changed.'

She sipped her wine, looking into the distance, the past pulling at her. 'Even after Max, I'd meet people. In playgrounds and cafés, on the street, and yet no matter who asked me out, the answer was always the same. You're the only man I've ever wanted, Dimitrios.'

He sat very still, his features inscrutable. But in the depths of his eyes she could see emotions—concern, resistance, disbelief.

It was another answer he didn't realise he was giving her. His obvious rejection of what she was saying made it crystal-clear how little he welcomed this confession.

'I was angry at you too, though,' she continued anyway. 'Angry that you were going on with your life, with other women, other friends, and no doubt you'd forgotten all about me.' She shook her head. 'So long went by that somehow I hoped my feelings for you had dwindled into nothing in the intervening years.'

He reached for his wine for the first time, taking a generous drink before quietly replacing the glass between them on the table. 'Go on.' His voice was a growl, scarcely encouraging.

'I can't fight this any more, Dimitrios. I don't *want* to fight it. I'm as much in love with you as ever, and last night just made it impossible for me to ignore it. Everything clicked into place for me. I love you.'

Silence fell, loud with expectation.

She waited, even when she knew that every second stretching between them made the waiting futile.

'Annabelle.' He sighed, standing up and coming round to her side of the table, leaning against it, his long legs kicked out in front of him. His citrusy cologne reached her nose, making her insides clench in instinctive recognition. 'You are...'

He paused, searching for the right words. 'An incredible mother, and a beautiful person. I respect you so much. And there's no one on earth I would rather be married to, raising a child with.

But this marriage isn't about love. For both our sakes, we need to be clear about that.'

She nodded jerkily, hating how close he was, hating that his answer was the opposite of what she wanted. Hating and loving him so damned much in that moment.

'You have been very clear,' she answered slowly. 'But now it's my turn.'

He was still, waiting. She reached for her glass, comforted by the feeling of the stem in her fingertips.

'I thought I could do this. Our marriage makes sense and, after what you've missed with Max, I wanted you to have proper time with him.' She drank to clear her throat.

'I'm glad.'

'I married you because I knew that if I said no you might have taken him away from me and I couldn't have handled that. I still couldn't.'

Tears filled her eyes; she blinked quickly.

'But the problem is, you've made everything too perfect.' She looked up at him, seeing him through the fog of her tears.

'And "too perfect" is bad?'

He wiped away one of her tears, but she flinched—the touch was too much. She couldn't bear his kindness; not if she was going to get through this.

'It can be.'

He made a noise of frustration. 'Why can't this work? Everything has been so great. We have fun together. We're attracted to each other. Why does that have to be a bad thing?'

His ability to see it so simply was the nail in the coffin for all her hopes, but still she needed to go through with this.

'You weren't the only one who made Lewis a promise before he died. I did too. I swore to him that I'd live my life for him and for me. He told me I deserved the fairy tale, the happily-ever-after.' A sob made the words thick. 'And this is so close, Dimitrios. You are everything I could ever want, for me and for Max, but if you don't love me too then I can't… I can't just pretend…'

'Shh,' he murmured, pulling her to stand against his chest, his lips pressing to the top of her hair. 'Please, don't cry.'

'I'm sorry, I didn't mean to, it all just hit me today. I think waiting to sleep together was a good idea, but it was also a bad idea, because last night when we made love I knew beyond a shadow of a doubt that for me it really was making love. I knew as we came together how much I love you. What we did means that much to me.' She reached for her hand and dislodged the yellow ring, placing it on the table. 'And for you, it meant something too. It meant having sex. With your wife, a woman you "respect", but that's all, isn't it?'

A muscle jerked at the bottom of his jaw. He didn't say anything, but then he didn't need to.

'This is… Everything is so beautiful.' She looked around, gesturing with her hand in a sweeping motion. 'You've made me feel like a princess in a fairy tale. It's not your fault that I forgot it was all just pretend. You've reminded me. You did everything you could to make me remember.'

He dipped his head in silent acknowledgement of that.

'But we're both trapped in this stunning, gilded cage. You would never have chosen this—me—would you? If it weren't for Max?'

His face was a forbidding mask.

'You don't have to answer,' she assured him, because his silence was answer enough. 'I know how you feel. You're doing everything you can for him, and for me, even though it means you're stuck living a life you would never have opted for.' She shook her head. 'And I'm sorry for that. I wish I could give you what you want—the kind of marriage that would make any of this worthwhile.'

'You think that's why I wanted to sleep with you?' he asked, disbelief etched in his tone. 'God, Annabelle, that wasn't me making the best of our marriage. It was the same insatiable need that drove me to you all those years ago. Everything else about this marriage might be a pretence but that isn't.'

She flinched, even though he was only confirming what she'd just said.

'I get it, but I've realised something today. I can't do half-measures. I can't make love with you when there's no love between us.'

He dropped his head forward, staring at the ground. 'Love isn't—and never has been—something I sought.'

Her smile was bittersweet. 'In my experience, you don't seek love, it seeks you.'

'Not me.'

'No,' she whispered, nodding, taking a step back from him. 'Definitely not you.' She wrapped her arms around herself, the reality of all this forming an ache low down in her abdomen.

'Please, wear this.' He reached for the ring but she held a hand up, shaking her head. 'It was a gift and it suits you.'

'It's very beautiful, but I don't think commemorating last night is a good idea.' She grimaced. 'Let's just…go back to how things were before, okay? We can forget it ever happened.'

Dimitrios wanted to rail against that. He felt trapped. Trapped between a rock, a hard place, an ocean, a tsunami and a wall of fire. He felt suffocated by indecision. He should say that he loved her. Just say the damned words and let this all go away. What difference would it make if he lied to her?

But he'd never do that, not even to relieve her suffering. Annabelle was brave and beautiful, telling him she didn't want a sham marriage. She wanted—and deserved—the real deal.

The guilt of the past few years was back, stronger than ever.

What would Lewis say if he knew what situation they were in—what situation Dimitrios had got them into?

God, what would Zach say?

He closed his eyes, his lungs hurting with the force of his breathing. 'Do you want a divorce?'

When he opened his eyes, all the colour had drained from her face. He ached to pull her into his arms but he knew the importance of the boundaries she was erecting. He had to respect them.

'Is that what you want?'

'No, Annabelle.' He dragged a hand through his hair. 'I don't want a divorce. I told you I wasn't going anywhere, and I meant that, one hundred per cent. But I don't want you to spend your life miserable and duty-bound, as you see it, to live with me.'

She tilted her face away from him, his outburst clearly hurting her. He swallowed a curse.

'I'm sorry. I just wasn't expecting this.'

Her eyes were haunted when they met his. 'You and me both.'

She chewed at her lip in a way he found far too distracting, given their current state of discord. 'I want what's best for Max.'

He frowned. 'I do too.' Uncertainty rippled inside him. 'But not if that's to your detriment.'

Her smile practically hollowed him out. 'Letting myself fall any further in love with you would definitely be detrimental to me. Treat me like a polite stranger and I'll be fine. Okay?'

A polite stranger. He stared up at the ceiling with a pain in his gut that wouldn't go away. A full forty-eight hours after Annabelle's confession, and Dimitrios's mood had gone from bad to worse.

Despite her pronouncement, she'd stayed in his room. 'Max will notice,' she'd said simply when he'd suggested he could move into a room down the hallway.

All of this was for Max. They were both in agreement on that. So here they were, polite strangers lying in his bed, on opposite sides of it, neither moving for fear of accidentally touching the other, despite the fact there was enough space between them to form a chasm.

As for sleep, it was a luxury that fell well beyond his grasp.

He shifted to look at her and something tightened low in his abdomen. He couldn't tell if she was asleep or not. It was possible the same thoughts were tormenting her, keeping her awake, an awareness of him like a form of torture, just as it was for Dimitrios.

But if she was pretending to sleep then it was logical to conclude she would continue to do so even if he moved. Stepping out of bed, he grabbed a shirt from the wardrobe and pulled it on, determinedly not looking back at the bed until he reached the door. Only then did he tilt his face a little, dark eyes that swirled with frustration finding Annabelle, looking for her, hoping to see—what?

She'd rolled over, turning her back on him.

She wasn't asleep, but she was closed off to him, and he suspected he deserved that.

CHAPTER TWELVE

IT WAS IMPOSSIBLE not to feel the contrast with last Christmas Eve. Annie stared around the beautiful living room, with the twelve-foot Christmas tree Dimitrios had organised, and felt a wave of sadness. On the surface, this was perfection. Everything was so lovely, but Annie's heart was more broken than it had ever been.

This house, the decorations, the setting... everything was so stunning. She and Max had spent Christmas Eve the year before watching a children's movie and eating turkey sandwiches, but she'd been...happy.

Not whole, exactly. She knew now that a Dimitrios-sized gap had always been inside her, but it had been easy to live with a gap. His absence hadn't been as bad, because there'd been an element of not knowing. It had been possible to keep some kind of fantasy alive, even when she'd never really given it much thought on a conscious level. There'd been a level of plausibility.

But not now.

Now she'd felt everything he had to give and it had brought her to the edge of who she was, forced her to see him as he was, and she loved him—all of him. His rejection had cut her deeply but, as with everything, Dimitrios had done it so well. No screaming, no shouting, no accusations. It was nothing like her parents' arguments, nothing like the kind of marriage she'd spent a lifetime fearing she'd find herself living in.

Dimitrios was too honourable for that. Too kind. He didn't love her but he cared—not for her, necessarily, but for people in general. He was trying to do the right thing for everyone.

Annie couldn't be the one who ruined this. Max deserved her to try, to put aside her own feelings again, to bottle them up and hold them deep inside herself, just as she had in the past. If she could do that again, then Max could have both his mum and his dad. But with Dimitrios here, a living, breathing person within easy reach, could she be sure she wouldn't weaken and stumble? What if she decided that something was better than nothing and gave into the temptation that was weighing down on her?

Perhaps she should have kept the ring after

all—as a reminder of how she'd felt the morning after, a reminder to keep her distance.

Annie brushed her fingertips over the pine needles of the tree, releasing a hit of that festive fragrance into the room. She lifted her fingers, inhaling, a stupid tear wetting the corner of her eye.

The Christmas Eve before, she'd been worried about everything, but her heart hadn't been heavy like this.

'Mummy?'

Mummy. How much longer would he call her that? Surely not long.

She took a second to surreptitiously wipe away her tear then turned, forcing a bright smile to her face. Max stood beside Dimitrios and, in keeping with their current arrangement, she forced herself to give him the briefest nod of acknowledgement before turning all of her attention back to Max.

'I was just wondering where you'd been,' she lied, crossing the room but stopping at least a metre short of the two of them. It was impossible not to notice how well-matched they were. They belonged together. Whatever it cost her personally, staying was the right thing to do. It would be so much harder than leaving. In leaving she would have had the space to heal, but here the cause of her pain was a constant presence. But that didn't matter. Max's smile pushed any sense of grief from her mind for a moment.

'We've been shopping.'

'Have you?'

'Uh-huh. Look.' Max pulled something from behind his back—a small box wrapped neatly in red. 'A present for you.'

Annie's heart turned over in her chest. 'You got something for me?'

'It was Daddy's idea. And Uncle Zach's.' Her heart twisted at the ease with which those two figures had become a part of Max's life—a daddy, an uncle. 'Besides, you always get me something.'

Now Annie couldn't continue to ignore Dimitrios without appearing rude, and she was determined that Max wouldn't pick up on any tension between them. Her own childhood had shown her what that felt like—she wouldn't have Maxi growing up in a war zone.

'That was very thoughtful of you.'

His eyes seemed to lock on to hers, trying to draw something from deep within her. He was silently asking a question, but she had no idea what answer to give him.

'I hope you like it,' Max said, pushing the present towards Annie.

'I'm sure I will.' She held it in her hands, feeling the weight of it, letting that tether her to the present. She would open it in the morning; she wasn't sure she could face it now.

'Daddy has some ideas for what we should do today.'

Annie's heart sunk to her toes. 'Does he?'

'He says we should make a pudding. He doesn't have a traditional recipe, and I told him we don't either, but apparently lots of people do, and we agreed that making a pudding should be our new tradition. What do you think, Mummy?'

Annie was lost. On the one hand, it was such a beautiful idea, a gift for their son to cherish, but on the other it was asking way, way too much of her. She stared at Dimitrios for a moment, all her hopes in tatters at her feet. But this was the life she'd chosen. Hadn't she just been thinking how Max was worth this sacrifice?

'Great, Max.' Her voice was over-bright. 'I just have to send a quick email and then I'll be right with you.'

Annie didn't need to send an email, but she definitely needed a moment to rally her courage before she could come and join the fun family activity Dimitrios and Max had planned.

'Mummy works a lot,' she heard Max explain as she left the room.

'Does she?' Dimitrios guided Max past the tree towards the kitchen, but his mind was on Annabelle with every step he took. Her face. Her eyes. The sadness he saw there. The same guilt that had been dogging him for years was exploding inside him now.

'Yeah, she has to.' Max sighed heavily. 'She always wants me to have stuff, but it's hard. So she works a lot, because that's how she earns money, and it means I get new shoes when I need them and stuff.' He looked down. 'My feet grow really, really, really fast.'

Dimitrios smiled despite the direction of his thoughts. He guided Max into the kitchen.

'I wish she didn't work so hard, though.'

'Oh?'

Dimitrios began to pull ingredients from the pantry. With only a moment's notice, his domestic staff had made sure they had everything they needed on hand for the start of the Great Pudding Tradition.

'Yeah.' Max came to stand beside Dimitrios and, when he pulled a bag of flour out, Max took it, helpfully carrying it to a place on the bench before returning for another item.

'Why is that?'

'Because she's tired all the time.'

More guilt slashed Dimitrios. Guilt and a sense of failed responsibility. But it was more than that. He grabbed for the sultanas and passed them to Max, a frown on his face.

'And I'm loud and busy, and I like to do stuff like go to the playground, but I don't always like to ask Mummy because I know she's tired and if I do ask her she'll say yes.'

Dimitrios nodded. 'You're considerate, Max.'

'Thanks.'

Dimitrios had missed so much. He'd missed so much of Max's life, and he'd missed Annabelle being a mum. He'd missed her tiredness and her happiness, her tears, her pleasure, her everything.

'Do we need aprons? They always wear aprons in cooking shows.'

Dimitrios nodded, distracted. 'Yeah, they're here somewhere. Why don't you have a look?'

Max rifled through doors and drawers and appeared with a pair of aprons a minute later. 'There's only two.'

'Okay, I'll go without.'

Max shrugged. 'Can you help me with mine?'

'Of course.'

He secured it around his son's back, folding it in half to fit, tying it loosely into a bow. They were almost finished measuring ingredients before Annabelle appeared by the door to the kitchen, her expression inscrutable, her hair pulled into a no-nonsense pony tail he found his fingers itched to muss. He looked away with a sense that he was falling off the edge of a cliff.

'We saved you an apron, Mummy.'

She stiffened, and Dimitrios understood—this was the last thing she wanted to be doing. Damn it, he'd regretted hurting her for seven long years, and now what? Their marriage was going to hurt her every single day. He couldn't do that. He couldn't live with this.

But what other option did they have? She was right—they were both trapped in this marriage he'd insisted on, trapped by their love for Max.

'Thanks, darling. I'll just make a cup of tea...'

'I'll make it,' Dimitrios offered, his eyes holding hers until something shoved him right in the gut. He felt it like a physical blow, but it wasn't. Everything around him was shifting.

'That's fine. You keep measuring.' Her smile was brittle, but when she looked at Max it softened. 'I won't be long.'

'You know what we need?' Max said happily. 'Christmas carols.'

He was evidently oblivious to the undercurrent of tension flowing between his parents.

'Christmas carols are a great idea, darling. Let me see what I've got.' Annabelle reached into her back pocket and pulled out her phone. Dimitrios frowned at the sight of it—so old and battered. How had he missed that? She pressed a button and some old jazz carols began to play, filling the kitchen with nostalgia and magic. But Dimitrios was only half-listening.

He went through the motions of making the pudding, following to the letter the recipe on his own state-of-the-art phone, noticing that Annabelle kept a careful distance from him at all times.

It was one of the longest days of his life. Both

adults were doing everything they could to make it special for Max, which meant they spent the whole day together as a family. The tension of being near Annabelle and not being able to touch her, not being able to make her smile, almost crushed Dimitrios.

When Max was finally asleep, he went in search of Annabelle. He didn't know how he knew where she'd be, but something drew him to the Christmas tree downstairs. He found her sitting on the floor with a glass of wine, her legs crossed, her eyes on the present Max had given her, a small frown on her face. She'd showered and was casually dressed, her face wiped of make-up, her blonde hair loose around her face.

His gut clenched again in a now familiar sensation.

He loved Max. That love had been easy and instantaneous. He'd taken one look at his son and known the child was a part of him and always would be. And Annabelle?

Everything inside him ground to a halt. His blood stopped rushing, his heart stopped pumping, his lungs ceased to inflate; he was completely still. Even the world seemed to stand as it was, refusing to shift with its usual motion.

'Annie…'

It was the first time he'd abbreviated her name. She jerked her face towards his, her eyes huge and for a second unguarded, so he saw the pain there, the look of loss.

It was a strange thing to inspire revelation but it was like a lightning bolt for Dimitrios. He looked at Annie and knew in that instant he would do *anything* to make her happy. Not just to make her happy because she deserved to be happy, but because her happiness was suddenly the most important thing in the world to him. Because, if she wasn't happy, he never could be. Because Annie had come to mean everything to him, and he'd been too mired in his suspicion of love and marriage to see what was right in front of him.

'I was just…' She turned away from him, the sentence trailing off. 'I don't know. Sitting here.'

Her sadness hit him in the chest but now his reaction didn't bother him. He understood why his body had been lurching, clenching and feeling so completely different for weeks now. It had been so much smarter than his brain.

'Max has had a good day,' he said gently, coming to sit beside her. She stiffened; he felt it. God, he'd been such a jerk. How had he missed something so obvious?

Because he'd been fighting it—Annie—since the first moment they'd met, when she'd been fifteen and the little sister of his best friend.

'He's had a great day,' she agreed.

'And you?'

She turned to face him, her eyes roaming his face, as though looking for something. 'It was nice to see Max so happy,' she said eventually.

He lifted his hand to her cheek; he couldn't resist it, cupping her skin there. She leaned into his caress for a moment and then jerked back, almost knocking her wine glass over. He reached past her, catching it, then straightened.

'You told me about your parents' marriage, and I told you about mine,' he began quietly, knowing he needed to get every word of this right. 'But I don't know if I ever explained how much my dad's behaviour affected me. I don't know if I made it clear to you that seeing my mum broken by how much she loved Dad formed a part of me that I have held on to my whole life. I had a daily reminder that love is bad. Love hurts. That formed my backbone; it changed me. And

I have never regretted that; I've never felt that my life was lacking in any way.'

Her eyes were huge. She moved, as if she was about to stand up, to run away from this conversation. He couldn't have that. He reached across, putting a hand on her knee. 'Hear me out. Just for a minute.'

Her eyes swept shut. She wanted to leave, he could tell, but she nodded just once, then reached for her wine glass, cradling it in her fingertips. 'Go on.'

He released a breath he hadn't realised he'd been holding. 'I don't know if you remember the first time we met?'

Her response was another short, sharp nod.

'I found you—'

'Don't lie to me,' she warned.

'I'm not lying. I found you captivating. I found myself thinking about you and, whenever Lewis talked about you, which was all the time—he was so damned proud of you, Annie—I listened with my whole body. I was glad when he said you had a boyfriend, because whatever hold you had over me wouldn't survive that. Except it did. I thought of you often, and I wondered about you, so I did the only thing someone like me *could* do—I went out of my way to avoid you. Whenever you were with Lewis, I steered clear. I controlled my reaction to you completely by not seeing you.'

She looked towards the tree, the shimmering lights catching her face in little blades of gold and silver.

'And then, after his funeral, I was weak for the first time in my life. I followed my instincts. It was *never* just sex for me, Annie. And no one else would have done. I needed *you* that night. Only you could put me back together again. Only you could make sense of the grief that had deluged me completely. I needed *you*.'

Her lips parted at his words but she kept her face averted, as though looking at him would be too much.

'You were so beautiful and innocent—so much more beautiful and perfect than I'd dared imagine. I think I knew even then that you were the one person on earth who could make me forgot how much I hated the idea of marriage and love. You were far too great a risk and I wasn't brave enough to take it.' He ground his teeth together, hating himself for the decisions he'd made then.

'I disappeared out of your life because I knew

if I weakened, even a little, I would want all of you—all of you for ever—and I'm not someone who does "for ever". You deserved so much better than me.' He groaned. 'What a coward I was. A foolish, selfish coward. I told myself I was protecting you by pushing you away, by saying all those awful things to you, but I was protecting my own stupid heart, making sure there was no risk you'd ever want me again.'

She turned to him then, her beautiful eyes showing sympathy—a sympathy he had no right to.

'I spent seven years consciously forgetting you, and I mean that literally—it was a conscious effort I made every damned day, not to think of you. Because you were all I wanted to think about, Annie. You're the only person I've ever met who's had this kind of hold over me and now I finally understand why.'

She mouthed the word, 'Why?' but no sound emerged.

'I love you,' he said simply. 'I have loved you since before I even met you, but that day you became a part of my soul. I don't know why, but there is something in you that answers everything in me, and I have fought that harder than I ever want to fight anything again.'

A juddering sound escaped her lips. 'I'm not going to take Max away from you, if that's what you're worried about,' she said quietly. 'I'm not going to ask you for a divorce. I meant what I said the other day. I'm committed to our marriage, because of Max—'

'This isn't for Max,' he interrupted, brushing his thumb over her lower lip. 'I could have moved to Sydney, set up across town from you, shared custody of him. This was never just about Max. It's been about my family—the woman I love and the child that love made. It's about us being together because that's how we belong. It's about you getting every happily-ever-after you deserve, just like Lewis said. This isn't guilt speaking, Annie, it's hope. Hope that you can forgive me, eventually, for the pain I put you through, for my useless foolishness when it came to you. It's hope, a hope that I probably don't have any right to hold, that you can let yourself love me without fear, without pain.'

She stared at him and every second that passed was like a weight being added to his chest.

'I always play to win. You probably know that

about me. I told myself I married you for Max. All along I've told myself this is for Max—but these last few days have shown me what a lie that was. Because Max is right here in my home, exactly where I wanted him, but with you being miserable and pulling away from me I can't be happy. I don't just want Max, I want you too, Annie. You're both a part of me.'

She stared at him, tears moistening her lovely eyes, the thick lashes clumping at the base.

'I love you,' he said simply, urgently. 'With all that I am. Not because of Max, not because of Lewis, but because of you, Annabelle Papandreo.'

She made a strangled noise and shook her head, and a part of him threatened to break. He needed to do more, to say more. How could he make this any clearer?

'You called this a gilded cage the other day. Well, yes. It is. I gilded it for you, because I wanted you to have everything imaginable. Because I love you. Every gift was chosen by me for your happiness. I wanted to give you everything because I was too scared to give you my heart—and I see now that's the one single thing you've ever wanted, the one thing that would have shown you how much you mean to me. Now the thing I'm most afraid of is that you won't believe me, or you won't trust me not to hurt you again. The gilded cage isn't our marriage, it's the idea of living a life without you in it.'

'Dimitrios—'

'You don't have to answer tonight. We've both waited seven years for me to stop being so obtuse. I can wait a bit longer. Just—think about what you want. And know how I feel about you.'

She closed her eyes; he hated that. He wanted to see her thoughts, to understand her emotions. But when she opened them again, she was smiling and shaking her head. 'I'm not going anywhere.' She repeated the words he'd once said to her, and his heart leaped.

'What does that mean?'

She laughed softly, tilting her head back. 'I love you,' she said with a lift of her shoulders. 'And it sounds like you love me too—a lot— and so, to my mind, that's kind of a Christmas miracle.'

He looked towards the tree, a grin breaking out on his face as he relaxed for the first time in a long time.

'Everything has been so perfect, Annie. None

of this was pretend. It was perfect because it was real.'

'Yes,' she agreed, leaning forward and brushing her lips to his. 'And it always will be.'

'Yes,' he promised, kissing her right back. 'You will live happily-ever-after. I promise you that now, with all that I am.'

'I believe you.'

'I was just thinking how perfect this has been.' Annie smiled as Dimitrios walked into the room. Christmas day was drawing to a close, and it had been the most blissful day of Annie's life. Max had loved his gifts, and Annie had adored her picture frame—with a photo of Max and her inside it—and the pudding they'd made had been the icing on the cake, a delicious tradition to take forward into all their future Christmases.

When she'd whispered to Dimitrios that she hadn't got anything for him, his eyes had glowed and he'd leaned forward and whispered in her ear, 'You are all the gift I require, Mrs Papandreo.'

But Dimitrios had a look on his face now that had her sitting a little straighter and placing her eggnog on the end table. 'What's the matter?'

'Nothing, I think.' A frown etched its way across his face. 'I just had the strangest conversation with Zach. He's coming over soon.'

'Here?' She glanced at her wristwatch. 'It's eleven o'clock.'

Dimitrios laughed. 'For Zach, that's when the night begins.'

'Of course,' she agreed. 'Well, it will be nice to see him, anyway.'

'I just pray he doesn't stay too long.' Dimitrios grinned, brushing his lips to Annie's. 'I have plans for you, my love.'

'And I hope they last all night...'

'All night? How about a lifetime?'

* * * * *

LET'S TALK
Romance

For exclusive extracts, competitions
and special offers, find us online:

- **f** facebook.com/millsandboon
- **◎** @millsandboonuk
- **𝕏** @millsandboon

Or get in touch on 0844 844 1351*

For all the latest titles coming soon,
visit millsandboon.co.uk/nextmonth

*Calls cost 7p per minute plus your phone company's price per
minute access charge

Want even more
ROMANCE?

Join our bookclub today!